THE TEXAS COWBOY'S BABY RESCUE

CATHY GILLEN THACKER

D0795010

MILLS & BOON

First Published in Great Britain 2018
by Mills & Boon, an imprint of HarperCollins*Publishers*
1 London Bridge Street, London, SE1 9GF

The Texas Cowboy's Baby Rescue © 2018 Cathy Gillen Thacker

ISBN: 978-0-263-26490-6

38-0418

MIX
Paper from
responsible sources
FSC® C007454

This book is produced from independently certified FSC™ paper to ensure responsible forest management.

For more information visit: www.harpercollins.co.uk/green

Printed and bound in Spain
by CPI, Barcelona

Chapter One

It was the day, Bridgett Monroe liked to say, that changed *everything*. She was on her way to work, same as always, when a puppy galloped out of the predawn shadows and dashed in front of her small SUV.

She slammed on the brakes, barely missing him, then watched as the mutt pranced around her vehicle, barking at her with ferocious urgency before looping back in front of her once again. The adorable beagle/golden retriever mix was splattered with dried mud and burrs, and dragging a tie-out chain and stake behind him.

Clearly, if she didn't do something, he was going to get hit.

Afraid to move her vehicle at all lest the two of them collide, Bridgett shoved her car into Park, turned on the emergency blinkers and got out.

"Hey there, little guy," she urged softly, kneeling down in front of the pup and holding out her arms in an attempt to coax him out of the path of her vehicle. "Why don't you come see me?"

He stared at her with liquid brown eyes, thinking.

"I won't hurt you, I promise. I just want to be your friend." Bridgett reached out to rescue the runaway pet.

To no avail. He eluded her grasp, jumped swiftly back out of reach and let out another commanding bark.

Tossing his floppy ears in the direction he wanted her to go, he headed on up the block, still dragging the tie-out chain and stake behind him. Periodically he looked back to see if she was following him.

Worried about what would happen if she left him to his own devices, Bridgett headed up the street after him. The cute little mutt let out a happy woof, raced over several lawns and crossed the street. He waited for her to catch up, then darted past a few more houses, out of the residential area into historic downtown Laramie, Texas, and behind the fire station.

The bays were empty, which meant the crew was out on an emergency run.

Too bad, Bridgett thought, as she stopped just short of the tall brick building. She could have used some help lassoing this frisky pup. Frowning, she glanced at her watch again, debating how much time she could really afford to devote to this when she had a car still parked in the middle of the street two blocks away, and patients in the hospital N-ICU who needed her, too.

And that was when she became aware of a whoosh of frantic activity as the pup dashed up to her once again, caught the leg of her nursing uniform pants between his teeth and pulled ferociously.

Determined, it seemed, to have her continue to follow him.

Curious, she did, the leg of her scrubs clamped in his jaws as he led her along the side of the big brick fire station. Over to a...*fairly large cardboard box*?

The pup let go abruptly and sat down next to the shipping carton, panting loudly. He stared up at her as if he expected her to know exactly what to do.

Taking a deep, bracing breath, Bridgett leaned over, cautiously opened up the loosely folded flaps and felt her heart stall with a mixture of shock and disbelief. "Oh, puppy," she whispered in startled dismay as she sank to her knees and reached inside. "No wonder you needed my help!"

ELEVEN HOURS LATER, the rugged Texas rancher who had been systematically avoiding all of Bridgett's calls and messages strode purposefully onto the maternity and pediatric floor of Laramie Community Hospital.

She wasn't surprised that the notoriously unsentimental rancher appeared to have come straight from the range. His short, curly, espresso-brown hair still bore the marks of the Resistol in his hand, his handsome face the burn of the spring wind and sun.

Nor was she surprised that he would want to have this conversation in person, rather than over the phone.

What she wasn't prepared for was the way her heart was suddenly pounding.

It's not as if he's all that much older. He'd only been five years ahead of her in school.

Or more successful. Professionally, both were at the top of their game. Although, she had to admit, given his rising success as a cattle breeder and land owner, he was likely a far sight wealthier.

Not that he flaunted that, either, she realized on a sigh as her knees went all wobbly. He was a man's man, through and through. The dusty leather boots on his feet were well broken in. And though there was nothing unique or expensive about his rumpled chambray shirt, it still cloaked his broad shoulders and muscular chest as if it was custom-made, and his faded Wranglers did equally showstopping things to his sinewy lower half.

Oblivious to the forbidden nature of her thoughts, Cullen McCabe slammed to a halt just short of her. His dark brows lowered like thunderclouds over mesmerizing navy blue eyes.

Her breath caught in her chest.

"Is this an April Fool's joke?" he demanded gruffly.

Feeling a little angry about how this all had transpired, too, she gestured at the infant slumbering on the other side of the nursery's glass window. The adorable newborn had a strikingly handsome face, ruddy skin, short and curly espresso brown hair and gorgeous blue eyes.

Just like the man standing in front of her!

She tilted her head back to better look into Cullen's face. "Does this look like a joke, McCabe?" Because it sure wasn't one to her! Or any of the emergency personnel who had been summoned to the scene of the abandonment.

Their eyes clashed, held for an interminably long moment. Cullen looked back at the Plexiglass infant bed, lingering on the tag attached to the front of it, marked Robby Reid McCabe?

His dark brow furrowed. "Why is there a question mark at the end of the name?"

Was he really going to play her and everyone else for a fool? Bridgett folded her arms in front of her. "Because we're not entirely sure of the foundling's identity."

"Okay, then…" He jabbed a thumb at his sternum. "What do I have to do with this baby? Other than the fact we apparently share the same middle and last names?"

Bridgett reached into the pocket of her scrubs and withdrew the rumpled envelope. "This was left beside the fire station along with the child. The infant was in a cardboard box, and the puppy—who had upended his tie-out chain—led me to him."

Cullen gave her another long, wary look. With a scowl, he opened the envelope, pulled out the typewritten paper and read out loud, "Cullen, I know you never planned to have a family or get married, and I understand that, maybe more than you could ever know, but please be the daddy little Robby deserves. And take wonderful care of his puppy, Riot, too."

Reacting a little like he had landed smack-dab in the center of some crazy reality TV show, like the one his cousin Brad McCabe had famously been on years ago, Cullen looked around suspiciously. Just as she might have in his situation.

To no avail. The only cameras were the security ones the hospital employed. "I don't see a puppy," he gritted out.

Aware she wouldn't have believed it, either, had it not actually happened to her that very morning, Bridgett returned wryly, "Oh, believe me, Riot was here." Wiggling and jumping around like crazy.

Cullen shoved a hand through his hair. "In the hospital?" His glare radiated swiftly increasing disbelief.

Bridgett flushed. That little irregularity could get her in a whole mess of hot water. Yet what choice had she had at the time?

Aware he radiated an intoxicatingly masculine blend of sun, horse and man, she stepped back. "It was just temporarily. My twin sister, Bess, came and took him to my apartment until you could get here to claim him."

"And the baby," Cullen added in disbelief.

"Actually," Bridgett told him, "because of the way all this went down, that is going to take a few days. And that's assuming you want Robby and Riot." She held up a hand before Cullen could interrupt. "If you don't, then social services is already working on a solution."

He stared at her, then the Plexiglas infant bed, then

back at her. "You really found this infant next to the fire station *in a cardboard shipping box*?"

Bridgett nodded as her heart cramped in her chest once again.

"I really did," she said softly, stepping a little closer. "Why else would I have tracked down your cell phone number and left ten messages over the course of the last eleven hours?"

Cullen fell silent once again and just shook his head.

Bridgett had an idea how he felt. She'd had most of her shift to deal with this, and she still couldn't get over both the miracle and the horror of it.

She had to keep reminding herself that despite the fact the several-days-old Robby Reid McCabe had been swaddled in a disposable diaper and a man's old chambray shirt, and his knotted umbilical cord was still attached when he was found, he really was okay.

And that was as much a godsend as the fact that she had been in the right place at the right time, for once in her life.

As Cullen stepped closer to the glass and gave the baby another long, intent look, Bridgett inched nearer and stared up at him. At six foot four, he towered over her five feet seven inches. Quietly, she explained, "Robby was apparently surrendered under the Texas Safe Haven law. Or attempted to be, anyway."

Cullen swung back to Bridgett, all imposing, capable male. "What's that?"

"Any infant sixty days old or younger can be surrendered—safely and legally—at any fire station, free-standing emergency medical care center, EMT station or hospital in Texas, but they are supposed to be left with an employee. Not just dropped off and left in the care of a dog who was staked nearby. Although, to Riot's credit, he did do a good job of insuring that Robby got quick aid."

Cullen rested a shoulder against the glass and folded his arms against his broad chest. "You found him?"

She nodded. "Fortunately, the baby was sleeping. From the looks of it, little Robby didn't even seem to know he had been abandoned. So he couldn't have been there very long at all." Thank heaven.

Cullen's expression radiated all the compassion Bridgett had hoped to see. "I'm sorry to hear that." He stepped forward, inundating her with the mint fragrance of his breath. His voice dropped another notch as his eyes met and held hers. "But unfortunately, I don't have any connection to this baby."

"Sure about that?"

He frowned at her. "I think I would know if I had conceived a child with someone."

"Not necessarily," she countered. Not if he hadn't been told.

Briefly, a resentment that seemed to go far deeper than the situation they were in flickered in his gaze.

He braced both hands on his waist, lowered his face to hers and spoke in a low masculine tone that sent a thrill down her spine. "I think I would know if I had slept with someone in the last ten or eleven months." He paused to let his curt declaration sink in. "I haven't."

Neither had she, ironically enough. Although she hadn't ever really been interested in having sex simply for the sake of having sex. She wanted it to mean something, the way it had with Aaron.

She wasn't sure a man as unsentimental as Cullen would feel the same. For him it might only be about satisfying a need as basic as eating and sleeping.

Studying her, he scoffed. "Obviously, you don't believe me."

Bridgett shrugged, aware this was becoming way too

personal, too fast. "It's not up to me to believe you or not," she returned lightly as Mitzy Martin, Laramie County's premiere social worker, walked up to join them, sheaf of papers in hand.

Not sure if they knew each other, Bridgett made introductions.

Laramie County Sheriff's Deputy Dan McCabe—one of Cullen's younger brothers—strode up to join them, too.

"Let's take this into a conference room," Mitzy said, leading the way down the hall.

Once the door was shut behind them, all four moved to take seats at the table. The windowless space was tight, especially with two big, strapping men in it, and Bridgett had to work to keep from brushing shoulders and legs with Cullen.

"Why are you here?" Cullen asked his brother.

Dan sent his older brother a sympathetic glance. "I volunteered due to the sensitive nature of the situation."

Cullen nodded his understanding, but he did not look happy. Briefly, he repeated what he had already told Bridgett, then asked in the same gruff tone he'd used with her, "Is there any way I can prove this baby isn't mine?"

Bridgett called on her training to answer what was essentially a medical question. "Not without the mother's DNA."

"So, until then?" he pressed.

Mitzy's answer was brisk. "Robby is going into foster care."

Bridgett's heart squeezed in her chest. Aware she was about to learn of an even more important decision, she looked at her friend hopefully. "Was my request granted?"

With a staying lift of her hand, Mitzy allowed, "Temporarily. As long as you understand that this child is not, and may not ever be, available for adoption."

Bridgett thought about the emotional connection she had already forged with the infant. The reservations she'd had up to now, about opening herself up to further heartache, faded completely. "I can handle it," she vowed to one and all. "Furthermore, I'll do as the note requested and take Riot, too."

CULLEN WOULD HAVE figured the social worker would be happy to hear that, since it meant her job here was done. Instead, Mitzy Martin looked as stressed as Bridgett Monroe had when he'd arrived at the hospital to confront her.

She leaned forward. "Are you sure, Bridgett? Up to now you've adamantly refused to consider fostering any child not available for adoption because you have a hard enough time saying goodbye to the babies in N-ICU and didn't think you could do it in your personal life, too." She reached over to take her friend's hand. "And I get that. We all do."

So, Bridgett Monroe had a heart as soft as her fair skin and bare pink lips. Cullen couldn't say he was surprised. Any more than he was surprised about his reaction to her. Stubborn, feisty women always turned him on.

"This is different," Bridgett said, color flooding her face.

"How?" Cullen asked, an answering heat welling up deep inside him.

"I know it sounds crazy…but I think I was meant to find these two."

It was all Cullen could do not to groan. The last thing he needed was another overly sentimental woman in his life. Even on the periphery. Yes, she was graceful and feminine. Pretty in that girl-next-door way, with her glossy, rich brown hair, delicate features and long-lashed pine-green eyes. She wore a long-sleeved white T-shirt beneath the blue hospital scrubs that seemed to emphasize, rather than hide, her svelte curves and long legs.

But she was also an emotional firebrand—at least, when it came to him. Jumping to conclusions. Pulling him in. Then shutting him out, just as quick.

He did not need those kinds of ups and downs.

Especially not now.

Mitzy and Dan exchanged a wary glance.

"Unfortunately, Bridgett," the social worker put in gently, "even if what you say is true, that this was all destined to happen the way it did, it doesn't mean your chances of fostering then adopting a baby on your own have changed. At least, as far as the department goes."

Cullen watched as disappointment glimmered in Bridgett's eyes.

Gently, Mitzy continued. "The district supervisor and the local family court judge who hears these cases want infants who are in search of permanent placement in a stable, *two-parent* home."

"But for every rule or policy there's always an exception that can be made, especially in special circumstances like these," Bridgett persisted resolutely.

"Yes." Mitzy chose her words carefully. "But I wouldn't count on that happening, long term."

Except Bridgett was, Cullen noted in concern.

With a sigh, Mitzy continued, "They're willing to make an allowance for Robby *temporarily* because you're a nurse and Robby is just a few days old with health issues that may or may not crop up, but—"

"Whoa," Cullen put in. "If there is any kind of risk, why not keep the baby in the hospital?"

Bridgett swung around, her elbow nudging his rib in the process. "Because the few problems he had upon admission have been treated. Hence, there's no reason to keep him here."

"So—" Mitzy looked at Dan "—unless there has been any further news on the law enforcement front...?"

Dan shook his head. "Sadly, not yet. But the Laramie County sheriff's department has sent information requests to all the hospitals, clinics and urgent care facilities in the state."

Cullen's gut tightened at the thought of all the people who would hear his name tied to this heartbreaking situation. The assumptions they would make about his character, and by default, the McCabe family, could be catastrophic.

He couldn't believe he was doing it again, bringing shame upon those closest to him.

"Is this going to be on the news?" he asked tensely.

"No," Mitzy said. "We don't want to scare off the birth mother if she does change her mind in the next few days and wants to come forward and reclaim her child."

Looking as shocked and horrified as Cullen felt, just considering the possibility. Bridgett cut in, "Would the Department of Child and Family Services really allow that to happen?"

Mitzy paused. "It's hard to say. There could be mitigating circumstances behind the mother's actions."

"Like what?" Cullen bit out, not surprised to find himself siding with Bridgett on this.

"Like she's suffering from postpartum depression and isn't thinking clearly," Mitzy suggested.

"The note she left with the baby seemed pretty clear-cut to me," Cullen said.

"In any case, we're all aware there has to be much more to this story than we know thus far," Mitzy explained. "So law enforcement and the medical community are all on alert for a woman coming in, having just given birth but without a baby to show for it. If anything the least bit suspicious occurs, we'll hear about it, pronto. And go from there."

Bridgett sat back in her chair, looking dejected again.

Cullen could imagine how the dedicated N-ICU nurse felt.

She'd found the abandoned infant and puppy, and the idea of giving Riot and Robby back to someone who had been unhappy or unbalanced enough to leave a baby alone in a cardboard box with only a puppy to guard it had to rankle.

It sure as hell did him.

"So, if you're sure this is what you want, Bridgett, even knowing it's only temporary..." Mitzy began.

Bridgett's expression turned fierce. "I am."

"And what about you?" Mitzy turned to Cullen.

Not sure what the social worker was asking, Cullen shrugged. "I just told Bridgett. There's no way on earth that Robby is my baby."

To his frustration, Mitzy looked as skeptical of that as Bridgett and his younger brother had. "Can you tell us who might *want to assign* paternity to you, then?" Mitzy asked.

Suddenly, all eyes were upon him once again. Cullen thought a long moment, then, unable to come up with anything, shook his head.

Mitzy pulled a pen from her bag, perfectly calm. Matter-of-fact. "So you're formally surrendering all claim to this infant, then?" She brought out another piece of paper.

Was he?

Cullen hadn't expected to do anything except come to the hospital, straighten out the situation and leave. However, seeing the newborn infant, reading the note, changed things. Made him feel that he just might be involved here.

How, exactly, he didn't know yet.

But he was a McCabe, as well as a Reid.

And unlike the Reids, McCabes did not shirk their obligations, familial or otherwise. So he was going to have to see this calamity through to its resolution.

Aware what Bridgett Monroe probably wanted him to say, so the way would be clear for her, he paused, then finally said, "No."

His younger brother Dan looked on approvingly, while sharp disappointment showed on Bridgett's pretty face.

Mitzy simply waited.

Cullen inhaled deeply, then directed his remarks to everyone in the room. "Someone left the puppy and the baby for me. Like it or not, that makes them my responsibility. At least until their real family is found or permanent arrangements can be made to give them a good home. So I'd like to keep tabs on the child while he's being fostered. Meet the dog." Who might have more of a connection to him than anyone except his brother yet knew.

Mitzy turned. "Bridgett? Is this going to be okay with you? Because if you'd rather your first ward be a child who has already been released for adoption, I would completely understand. And so would everyone else at the department."

For the first time since he'd laid eyes on her, Cullen saw Bridgett falter. She turned to glance at the papers that would make her the baby's temporary foster mother and, for a second, looked so vulnerable he couldn't help but feel for her. Pushing aside the temptation to take her in his arms and comfort her, he swallowed hard, reminding himself this situation was complicated enough as it was.

Bridgett drew herself up, raised her chin and looked Mitzy straight in the eye. "I can handle this," she vowed. *Could she?* Cullen wondered.

Chapter Two

"You really don't have to walk us to my SUV," Bridgett said half an hour later, as she got ready to go.

Cullen was clearly skeptical. "You're saying you could easily manage all this on your own?"

Bridgett looked at the messenger bag she took to work, the diaper bag filled with emergency essentials, and the swaddled infant she was about to pick up. He had a point. It was a lot.

"Okay." She handed him both bags and her vehicle keys, then gently picked up little Robby.

She'd handled hundreds of newborns in her career. Cuddled and given medical aid and taken care of their emotional needs for as long as they were in the N-ICU.

But this was different. It had been from the first moment she'd gathered the little infant in her arms.

She felt connected to this child, heart and soul.

As if she were already his mother.

"But that's all the help we need," Bridgett continued firmly. "Once I get to my apartment and you meet the puppy, to see if that sparks anything, I'll be able to handle it from there."

The only problem, she noted ten minutes later as she pulled up in front of her nondescript brick apartment building and saw a furious man pacing outside, was that she still had a few more wrinkles to iron out.

Cullen emerged from his pickup truck. He nodded at the short and stocky man storming their way. "Who's that?"

Her heart sank as she stepped from the driver's seat and faced off with the man who had just been peering in her apartment windows. "My landlord, Amos Stone."

The gray-haired man marched closer. "Miss Monroe! Do you have *a dog* in your apartment?"

Too late, Bridgett realized she should have found another emergency solution that morning. One that hadn't involved spiriting a dog who'd had no place in the hospital to yet another place he was absolutely forbidden to be. She fixed the building's owner with her most winning smile. "I can explain."

Her landlord did not think so. "Your lease explicitly says *no pets of any kind* allowed. Ever."

"I know." Bridgett reached into the car to gather Robby in her arms. "But—"

"No buts," the older man huffed. "You're out of here! Effective immediately."

Cullen stepped forward. "Surely there's some middle ground here," he beseeched cordially, on her behalf.

Amos Stone glared. "Nope. Twenty-four hours to get everything out, or I start formal eviction proceedings. And that mangy mutt goes right this instant. Or I call animal control to take him for you!" He stomped off.

Able to hear the barking from inside her unit, Bridgett handed Robby over to Cullen, then hurried to unlock her front door. What she saw, as the pup barreled toward her and leaped into her arms, was even more dismaying.

Riot had pushed aside the temporary barrier she'd set up between her small galley kitchen and the rest of the unit. He'd wreaked havoc throughout the apartment, knocking pillows off the sofa and upending plants, lamps and a basket of clean laundry. He'd also had several accidents on the wood floor.

Apparently being left alone had stressed the poor little guy out.

But now that the puppy was in her arms again, he was quiet, cuddly and clearly exhausted.

Cullen stood beside her, a drowsy Robby held against his broad chest. He looked around, surveying the damage. "What next?" he said.

Outside the window, she saw her landlord standing next to his car, phone to his ear. She headed outside again, to her vehicle, and Cullen followed. "Mr. Stone is probably on the phone with animal control right now. So we need to get Riot out of here."

Cullen inclined his head toward the slumbering infant. "Want to switch?"

"Um…let's not rock the boat just yet."

Especially since Robby looked as if he were in baby nirvana. She nodded at the safety seat that had been installed in the backseat of her SUV. "If you can settle Robby back in that, I'll hand off Riot to you and then get the baby strapped in."

Cullen did as she asked and then took the dog from her. "Where do you want the pup?" he asked.

Good question. To have Riot on the loose while she was driving and Robby was strapped in a car seat did not seem like a good idea.

Cullen understood her indecision. "Why don't I put him in my truck and drive him wherever you're going next?"

If only she knew where that was, Bridgett thought, opening the door on the driver's side to let the pleasant spring breeze circulate through the interior of the car.

For the next few minutes, they remained next to her SUV while she scrolled through the hotel listings on her phone and made a few quick calls.

"Any luck?" Cullen asked, after the third.

Disappointed, Bridgett shook her head. "None of the inns in the county allow pets."

Still holding the puppy against his chest, he used the index finger to tilt his hat a little higher on his forehead. "Doesn't your family own a ranch?"

"The Triple Canyon. My younger brother, Nick, and his wife, Sage, live there now, but they're currently putting a commercial kitchen in the ranch house so Sage can do the majority of the baking for her café-bistro on the premises. So they are at Sage's old one-bedroom in town with their two kids for the next three months."

He squinted down at her thoughtfully. "What about your twin sister?"

"Bess lives in the same building I do."

"So that's out."

"Right."

He studied her. "There's no one else in the area you could call upon in an emergency? Other family?"

Yes and no, Bridgett thought. "I've got two more siblings. My older brother, Gavin, and Violet and their two kids live in a shotgun house here in town that is already bursting at the seams. And my sister Erin and Mac are living in the Panhandle now, with their brood, so although they *would* take me in, I can't leave the county with Robby until everything is straightened out."

He edged close enough that she could smell the soap and sun-warmed-leather scent of him. "Friends, then?"

"The ones who live in houses all have kids and pets of their own, and the ones who don't live in apartments."

Cullen shrugged. "You could board the puppy at the

vet clinic in town temporarily or turn him over to the animal shelter."

"No!" The force of her response stunned them both.

Bridgett drew in a bolstering breath. "If it hadn't been for Riot's determination to get my attention, I never would have known Robby had been abandoned at the fire station. Who knows how long it would have been before he'd been rescued? Plus, the note specifically said the mother wanted the two of them to stay together. I intend to honor that."

"Do you even know anything about caring for a dog?"

Irked by his doubt, she tilted her chin at him. "No. But I'm sure I can learn. I just made an offer on a house, so all I need is a short-term solution that will hold us until I move."

He regarded her with new respect. "You're buying a home?"

Apparently, real estate was a language they both spoke. She nodded, forcing herself to relax. "An adorable little bungalow here in town. I'm just waiting for my mortgage application to be approved. Which unfortunately rules out renting another place. No one's going to want me in and out for just a couple of weeks."

"Well, since you are clearly out of options..." Cullen gave an affable shrug. "You could bring Robby and Riot to the Western Cross."

Bridgett blinked. "Stay with you? At your ranch?"

He nodded.

She crossed her arms and glared up at him. "Why would you want to do that?" she blurted out.

He regarded her calmly. "To fulfill my moral obligation, and to preserve my reputation and that of the McCabe family, of course."

CULLEN COULD SEE it wasn't the explanation Bridgett wanted. Which was too bad, because the blunt truth was the only reason he was prepared to give. "I've got a virtual cattle auction coming up in ten days. My first at the Western Cross ranch. If people think I am unreliable on any level, they're not going to buy livestock from me. So it's to my advantage, and yours, to get this resolved as soon as possible. And maybe if we're all together I'll be able to more quickly figure out who would have wanted me to be responsible for all this."

"Makes sense. I guess."

He continued looking her in the eye. "I also don't want to embarrass Frank and Rachel or any of the rest of my family." Thanks to his mom, and the way she had selfishly kept his paternity a secret, for years, so she wouldn't have to share him, they had already been through enough.

Bridgett went still, for a moment giving him a glimpse of the woman she was, at heart. "You call your parents by their first names?"

His attention drifted to her mouth. "Rachel is my stepmom. And Frank didn't come into my life until I was sixteen."

She bit her lip, her gaze glued to him. "That explains the Rachel. But Frank...?"

He shrugged, wishing he could table the urge to take down her hair and run his fingers through the thick, silky waves. "I never got the hang of calling him Dad."

She moved closer. "Did he want you to call him Dad?"

"We never discussed it," he said curtly. And he sure wasn't going to dissect his tumultuous early years with the nosy nurse in front of him. "So," he said, bringing the conversation back around to the current trouble at hand. "Are you going to take me up on my offer or not?"

She looked down at the baby, who was beginning to stir, and sighed. "I'm not sure if I'll stay the night or not, but I'll follow you out there, assess the situation and then figure out what I'm going to do."

Not exactly a yes. But likely the closest he would get.

He gave her the address to put into her navigation system in case they got separated, and then they took off. Twenty minutes later, they were turning beneath the archway to the Western Cross ranch. Both sets of vehicle headlamps swept over the live oaks lining the drive, the fenced pastures filled with cattle and the cluster of brand-new state-of-the-art barns and stables. Finally, he drew up in front of the ranch house and parked behind the Laramie Animal Clinic van.

His good friend, and recent widow, Sara Anderson stepped out. It was hard to tell whether the pale, drawn hue of her face was due to grief over the sudden loss of her soldier husband or the nausea associated with the first trimester of pregnancy. But he appreciated her willingness to help them out today.

He picked up Riot and met her in the middle of the circular drive. "Thanks for coming," he said.

The willowy blonde smiled, kind-hearted as always. "No problem." Sara studied Riot with a clinician's unerring eye, stroked him beneath the chin. "This the little runaway?"

"It is." And though it had been years since he had held one, Cullen experienced the lure of a puppy all over again.

Bridgett parked and got out, too, a fussy baby Robby in her arms. Cullen made introductions. "Sara Anderson, Bridgett Monroe. Sara's a neighboring rancher and the veterinarian who sees to all of my cattle and horses."

Bridgett nodded. "Sara and I talked at the county's High School Career Fair last fall. And we also both volunteer at the West Texas Warriors Assistance nonprofit."

"Ah, then no introduction necessary." Indeed, the two

women looked surprisingly chummy. He hadn't thought about them being friends. But then, he didn't spend a lot of time socializing with anyone outside the cattle business.

Sara moved an electronic wand over the pup, between his shoulders and neck and from side to side. Then over the rest of his body.

"Anything?" Cullen asked.

"No." Sara frowned. "I thought he might be a little too young for a microchip, but I wanted to be certain. There were no tags on his collar?"

"No."

"That's too bad. I'd like to know more about him." She opened up the back of her van and pulled out a medium-sized plastic crate with a metal-grill door. "The food, dishes and leash you requested are all in there. You're also going to need to make sure he gets started on all his vaccinations, ASAP."

"I'll make an appointment."

"Good." Sara grinned, tossing Cullen a bottle of puppy shampoo. "And you might want to give him a bath while you're at it."

Grinning, Cullen caught the bottle with one hand. "Thanks, Sara."

Sara paused to greet little Robby, who was wide-eyed and squirmy. "Bridgett? Good luck with the baby. I heard about the situation." She frowned, shaking her head. "I hope you get to keep him."

Abruptly looking like she might burst into tears at any moment, Bridgett nodded. "I want what's best for them both," she said thickly, the strain of the day showing on her pretty face. "And I appreciate your help with Riot."

"It was my pleasure," Sara said with a warm smile. "And if you need anything else, just ask." Then she climbed back into her van, gave a parting wave and took off.

Silence hung heavy between them as they stood there together, cradling puppy and baby.

Bridgett looked up, wordlessly scanning the compact century old farmhouse, whatever she was thinking at that moment as much a mystery to him as the emotion resonating in her dulcet tones.

"So, this is where you live," she said.

Chapter Three

"For the last ten and a half months, it has been," Cullen admitted as they moved inside.

He hit a button on the keypad by the door, and the place lit up. "And before that?" Bridgett prodded, trying to recall what she'd heard.

He led her through the foyer and shut the door behind them. "Oklahoma, for two years."

They were standing close. Almost too close. Bridgett swung around to face him, stepping back a pace in the process. She was acutely aware she really didn't know much about Frank McCabe's eldest son at all—and she wanted to know more, because of the situation they were in. Noting he looked as inherently masculine as he smelled—like sun and soap and leather—she searched the rugged planes of his face. "And prior to that, where were you?"

The grooves on either side of his sensual lips deepened. "Colorado for eighteen months, Nebraska for four years."

"Nebraska. Wow, you must have really liked it there."

He studied her, as if trying to decide how much farther he wanted this discussion to go. "It's the second-largest cattle-producing state in the country, and I had two different ranches. A small one in the north for about twenty-six months, a larger one in the south, for about the same amount of time."

"Which you purchased after starting out here, correct?" Her feminine instincts on full alert, she pushed on, curious to hear about the time he'd spent outside of Laramie County. "Somewhere in the Panhandle?"

His gaze roved her upturned face. He looked at her for a long beat. "How do you know that?"

She flushed under his intense scrutiny. "My sister Erin and her husband, Mac, mentioned it when they moved up there for his work."

He continued holding her gaze for a brief but electrifying moment that swiftly had her tingling all over. "Hmm."

"Mac said you were a rancher to watch."

Cullen shifted the exhausted puppy in his arms, cradling it to his broad chest. "I don't think Wheeler was too fond of me back then," he pointed out. "I outbid him on a property he wanted for his wind energy turbines."

Bridgett grinned. "I'm sure Mac forgave you." If there was one thing her brother-in-law respected, it was business acumen and skill.

A wave of unexpected contentment flowing through her, she snuggled the sleepy Robby, breathing in his sweet baby scent. "Speaking of family, though, yours must be happy to have you back in Texas again."

His expression darkened and the corners of his lips slanted downward. "They are."

"Are you?" Curiosity won out over caution yet again. "For the moment."

Which meant what? He had one foot out the door? Was getting ready to bolt again?

Not that it was any of her business what his future plans were. Once the current mystery was solved, anyway. She knew what her future was—it was right here in Laramie County with Robby and Riot.

"So." Bridgett forced herself to concentrate on their surroundings. She inclined her head toward the front two rooms of the thousand-square-foot first floor. The one on the right sported a wall of what appeared to be security monitors showing various areas of the ranch, while the other room was outfitted with a large, masculine mahogany desk, a comfortable chair, built in bookshelves and sleek computer equipment. Framed diplomas and awards adorned the whitewashed wood-paneled walls. "I gather this is where you do all the Western Cross ranch office work."

"Yep. And there's never any shortage of it." He moved forward, leading the way past an iron-railed staircase to the living room in the rear, which also had an open layout. She paused to admire the rustic fireplace, a big comfy sofa and the state-of-the-art entertainment center.

After getting a cursory glimpse at the pristine eat-in kitchen, she followed him to a screened-in porch, complete with cushioned furniture and a chain-hung swing. It overlooked a stone patio and built-in barbecue grill as well as an impressive view of the ranch.

"This, I am guessing, is where you hang out when you're not working." She tried not to think about how intimate it would be, sharing such a cozy space, and failed. "And maybe entertain." She pushed the words through the abrupt tightness of her throat.

He swung back to face her, looking as intrigued by her as she was by him. "Yes to the first. No to the latter."

Good heavens, her pulse was pounding. She moved slightly away. Pretended to stare out the windows at the fields beyond.

She spun back to face him, pretending a tranquility she couldn't begin to feel. "You don't entertain?"

Gesturing for her to follow, he moved back inside toward the centrally located staircase. "I give tours of the ranch to business associates by request. That's it." He paused on the first stair. "Why? Is that a high priority for you?"

"Not really. I've been spending all my time these days working extra shifts so I could save up enough for the down payment on a house. Which I have finally done."

Upstairs were three modestly decorated bedrooms, decked out in the same masculine gray-and-white color scheme as the rest of the home, and a full bath off the hall featuring a single pedestal sink, a private water closet and a tiled bathtub/shower combo big enough for a man of his size. "So, what do you think?" He shifted a restless Riot a little higher in his arms. "Will you-all be comfortable here tonight?"

In terms of creature comforts? Yes. In terms of having him sleeping just down the hall from her? Not so much. Yet what choice did she have? She had to make do until she had a better solution worked out.

"Absolutely. If you're sure it's going to be okay with you, too?"

He looked at her a long moment. A myriad of emotions came and went on his ruggedly handsome face. "We'll make it work," he said cryptically. And in that moment, as they headed back downstairs, she knew they would.

WHILE BRIDGETT CARRIED the baby and the diaper bag into the family room, Cullen headed outside with the puppy.

Thirty minutes later, she and Robby found them on the screened-in porch. The freshly bathed Riot was getting a rubdown with a towel and she smiled. "He has a lot more white fur than I realized."

"Yeah, I thought he was mostly brown, too." Laugh lines appeared at the corners of his eyes. "Guess a lot of it was mud. Robby okay?"

Trying not to think how easily she and Cullen meshed in the mom and dad roles, she nodded. "He took his bottle like a champ. Now all he has to do is burp a time or two, and I'll be able to put him down again."

Cullen brought two stainless steel bowls of food and water over and set them in front of where Riot was leashed to the railing.

The puppy stared at both.

"I know you have to be hungry," Cullen said, kneeling down to pet the mutt's head.

Riot still didn't touch the food.

Cullen took some kibble into his hand and offered it that way.

Riot hesitated, then inched closer, nudging Cullen's palm and finally eating a few small pieces. Cullen offered the bowl again, but when the pup once again refused, he was forced to go back to the hand-feeding method.

"Are all puppies that fussy?" she asked, walking back and forth, gently patting Robby on the back.

"I wouldn't know. I only had the one when I was a kid."

Bridgett caught the low note of emotion in his voice. "What happened to him?"

"He died at age nine. Cancer."

Clearly, Cullen still missed him. "You never got another?"

Another shake of his head. "Initially, I wasn't in a position where I could get another dog. After that—" he shrugged "—I was too busy ranching."

Robby gazed over at Cullen, mesmerized by the low

timbre of his voice. As was she. "Too busy?" she asked lightly, inclining her head at Riot. "Or too leery of giving your heart away to another little cutie like this?"

Cullen's head came up. As he exhaled, his broad shoulders tensed, then relaxed. "Too busy fixing up ranches, adding to my herd and moving from place to place."

"How big a spread do you want?" she asked, edging closer.

Cullen set the empty bowl aside, then led the still-leashed Riot over to the grass. "Minimum, ten thousand acres and a couple thousand head of cattle."

"Maximum?"

He shrugged. "Frank has fifty thousand acres on the Bar M."

"You'd like to equal your family's ranch?"

He nodded, solemn now. "Yeah, I would."

There was something oddly sentimental about following in his father's footsteps that way. Especially coming from such an unsentimental man. She looked out at the fenced acres, all of them spring-green and lush after plentiful March rains. "How many acres do you have here?"

Noting Riot had finished his business, Cullen praised him and patted him on the head. "Four thousand."

"So you have a way to go." She watched the puppy and man amble back onto the patio.

"I'll get there," he said confidently.

She'd bet he would.

In fact, she'd bet he would get just about anything he wanted. Good thing it wasn't her.

BRIDGETT AND CULLEN had dinner together and got the baby and puppy settled, then Cullen excused himself to go check on one of his prize bulls. Bridgett used the momentary quiet to hit the shower and change into a pair of light gray yoga pants and a long-sleeved light blue T-shirt.

That done, she settled on her bed and began making a to-do list for the following day, including all the notifications she had to take care of that very evening. Two and a half hours later, she was still working on the last and most important one. Aware Robby would be waking again soon, and would need to be fed when he did, she headed back down to the kitchen.

Cullen was seated at the kitchen table, laptop in front of him and what appeared to be business materials all around him. To her surprise, he appeared to have had a shower, too. But he had put on jeans and a black body-hugging T-shirt that let her know just how taut and muscular his body was. Clearly, he didn't sleep in jeans. Those were for her benefit, just like her yoga pants, instead of pj bottoms, were for his. She wondered if he slept in that shirt or went bare chested. Not that she should be conjuring up a mental image of him in boxers or briefs in the first place.

Her pulse kicking up a notch, Bridgett remained in the portal. Her face bare of all makeup, her freshly shampooed hair spilling about her shoulders in damp waves, she felt oddly defenseless. The situation suddenly way too intimate.

"Okay if I come in long enough to warm up a bottle?" she asked lightly.

He glanced up from the laptop in front of him, his gaze raking lightly over her from head to toe. Sensual lips curved into a ghost of a smile, he encouraged her to come in with a tilt of his handsome head. "*Mi casa* is you-all's *casa*…"

Temporarily, Bridgett reminded herself. Very temporarily.

She could not share close quarters with a man she

found this attractive. Not for long, anyway. Not without something ridiculously sexy and impulsive happening.

"Not for much longer if the solution I have been working on all evening comes to fruition."

Was that disappointment she saw etched on his handsome face?

He got up, suddenly. Went to the fridge, got a bottle of water, then held the door open for her so she could help herself, too. "How are things going up there?" His voice was low, polite.

She moved past to retrieve a premade bottle of formula, being careful not to touch him. She inhaled the clean, soapy scent of him. The minty smell of toothpaste. He hadn't shaved and the evening beard shadowing his face gave him an even more ruggedly masculine air.

Aware she hadn't answered his question yet, she smiled. "Both little fellas are still sleeping, but Robby should be waking up soon for another feeding, so I figured I would get ahead of the game and warm the bottle."

He tilted his head, his gaze drifting over her lazily, creating little sparks of awareness. "Before all hell breaks loose," he guessed.

Because she had no bottle warmer—yet—she filled a bowl with hot water and set the bottle in it. "I haven't noticed anything being out of control this evening." She adapted a militant stance. "If you discount the tiff with my landlord."

He flashed a teasing grin. "That's because, for the most part, there's been two of us and two of them."

It was so true she didn't want to think—or was it worry?—about that. Adopting the confident, cheerful air she usually used to tackle the problems in life, she asked, "What time do you usually get up and out of here in the morning?"

"Before dawn, usually, but tomorrow I'm planning to hang around here and do office work, at least initially." Seeing her unease, he murmured, "I also usually grab breakfast with the guys at the bunkhouse, but I could cook you breakfast." He shrugged. "If that will help you out."

There was a limit to how far she wanted his gallant involvement to extend. The vibe between them was far too personal already. "Or we could each cook our own," she said pleasantly. Another spark of tension flickered between them, and she felt her breath catch in her throat.

"Independent, hmm?"

She swallowed hard, then shot back firmly, "Like you're not."

He chuckled, a deep rumbling low in his throat. Then he slowly ravished her with his gaze, as if he found her completely irresistible. "Is that why you wanted to adopt a baby on your own?"

Trying not to think how physically attracted she was to him, too, Bridgett checked the formula on the inside of her wrist. Still cool. She added more hot water to the bowl and set the bottle back inside.

"I never said that solo adopting was my first choice."

Intimacy shimmered between them as he took up a station opposite her. The brooding look was back on his face. "But you're doing it?"

She leaned back against the counter, her hands braced on either side of her, not sure why his opinion mattered so much.

She sighed, figuring it wouldn't hurt to confide this much. "Only because I stupidly gave up the one shot I had at a happy family life."

His brow quirked and he shifted closer.

Which didn't mean she had to explain further. But, for reasons she couldn't understand, she wanted him to know.

"I was in love with a fourth-year medical student while I was in nursing school. He was headed back to Utah, where he was from, to do his residency, and he wanted us to get married before he left, start having kids right away. I still had another two semesters to go and I wasn't ready. But Aaron saw no reason to wait if we loved each other. So he gave me an ultimatum." Refusing the crazy urge to take refuge in Cullen's strong arms and rest her head against his broad chest, she continued. "Thinking he would become more reasonable over time, I refused."

Dark gaze skimming hers intently, he moved closer still. "Didn't work out?"

Her heartbeat quickened at the unexpected compassion in his low tone. "He married someone else within a few months of our breakup."

"Still married?"

Bridgett nodded. "Happily. They have six kids and another on the way." Six kids who could have been hers.

His brow knotted. "Wow."

"Yeah."

Silence fell between them.

"Still wishing it was you?"

Not the way he thought.

"Not really," she replied honestly. "I wouldn't want to leave my family, be that far away from Texas." She locked eyes with Cullen, not ashamed to admit it. "But I do regret giving up my one shot at marriage, especially knowing it might never come again."

His expression guarded, he said, "You're selling yourself short."

Finding his low, grumbling voice a bit too determined—and too full of sexual promise for comfort—she returned, "How do you know?" Who was he to give her advice on her love life or lack thereof? "Especially since you're not known to be the most sentimental guy around!"

Ooh, she should not have said that. But he was goading her. Making her feel foolish in the way he kept looking at her.

He came close and, if she was not mistaken, looked very much like he wanted to make love with her then and there. A wicked grin deepened the crinkles around his navy eyes.

She felt as if she'd just waved a red flag in front of a bull.

"You think not?" he prodded.

Bridgett huffed. "I do." Knowing it was a dangerous proposition to have him that close to her—because she did desire him more than anyone who had come before—she moved away. Feeling hot color flush her cheeks, she enunciated as clearly as possible, "I also know that, unlike you, I believe very strongly in destiny or fate or whatever you want to call it. And that destiny brought Riot and Robby—"

He prowled toward her. "And me."

Ignoring the fierce sense that he was about to put the moves on her, she stubbornly finished her sentence. "Into my life. So if this is what's meant to be for me, I'll take it."

In one smooth motion, he took her all the way into his arms. Pressed her against him in a way that left her reeling and lowered his lips to hers. "So will I," he said.

IN INVITING HER to stay, Cullen hadn't meant to do anything but clear his own reputation and help Bridgett out. He hadn't figured what it would be like to have her, and the baby and puppy, in his home. Or how much he would quickly come to admire her fierce desire to help others, even as she shortchanged herself.

Was it possible she really had no idea how beautiful and desirable she was? How worthy of having?

It seemed so. And that was something he couldn't let stand unchallenged, as all thoughts of being a gentleman fled. She had to know how captivating she was. So he did what he'd been wanting to do since they had first caught sight of each other; he kissed her. Kissed her to discover how soft and supple and sweet-tasting her lips were. Kissed her to fulfill a yearning deep inside him that he hadn't known existed.

And, most of all, he kissed her to show her that they could simply enjoy each other without the false illusion of love or emotional promises that would most likely end up being short-term.

But he was the one who was surprised. Because this kiss, holding her like this, didn't feel like any normal clinch. It felt different. Unique. *Amazingly* unique, as it turned out.

And who was the naive fool now?

BRIDGETT HAD KNOWN from the moment that she walked into the kitchen, hours after dinner, that a kiss, a touch, an embrace, something might be coming. It was in the way he looked at her. The way she felt when she looked at him.

It was in the leftover adrenaline still sizzling nonstop in her veins. In the building emotions and aftereffects of this crazy, crazy day. Of having her dreams start to come true, but not. Of realizing she *still* wanted it all. Maybe could have it all. If only she could find the right man.

She never would have imagined it could be Cullen Reid McCabe. But then, she had never really imagined kissing him. Now that she had, well, suffice it to say her whole world had turned upside down.

Which was why it was a very good thing when a short,

loud, high-pitched cry split the silence of the ranch house. Followed by a single urgent bark.

Destiny once again, Bridgett thought, pulling away from the sexy cowboy who held her in his arms. But this time it was telling her *not* to go down this particular path.

Chapter Four

"So, he kissed you?" Bess asked the next morning at Bridgett's apartment.

"Shh!" She cast a look over her shoulder at the guys helping her move out. "Yes."

Her sister grinned. "Did you kiss him back?"

"What does that matter?" she whispered, flushing. Unfortunately, yes, she had kissed him back! For way too long a time! "It was obviously a mistake."

Bess grinned again. "Sure about that? From what I've seen, he's very sexy. Well regarded in the community. Single and obviously interested in you. *And the baby.*" She taped shut another box. "And where is Riot, anyway?"

"With Cullen. He took him to work in his truck." Bridgett selected the clothes she needed to take with her when she left versus those that were going into storage. "Well, the puppy couldn't be here, obviously, after what happened yesterday with the landlord, and *quit* looking at me like that!"

Bess chuckled. "What is it they say? Life happens while you were making other plans. Well, while you were trying, rather unsuccessfully, I might add, to adopt a child on your own, a baby and a puppy and a kind, great-looking cowboy all drop in your lap!"

Bridgett thought about what a great and gallant thing

it was that Cullen was doing. Not just inviting her to stay with him at his ranch but helping her out with both infant and puppy, too. She looked at her sister. "It's almost crazy spooky, isn't it?"

"*Fated* is the word you're looking for."

Bridgett paused. "It may seem that way."

"I'm telling you…it most definitely is." Bess pointed at the well-dressed Realtor coming up the walk. "Oh, and speaking of fate…"

Bridgett met Jeanne Phipps at the door. "Did you get the answer from the sellers?"

"Yes." Jeanne flashed a regretful half smile. "Unfortunately, Bridgett, it's not the one you want to hear."

"WHAT'S WRONG?" CULLEN ASKED, coming through the ranch house door at five that evening.

Bridgett eased the sleeping Robby into the carrier sitting on the kitchen island, strapped him in and brought him into the adjacent family room. "What do you mean?" She knelt down to greet an equally tuckered-out Riot.

He nuzzled her palm, licked it once and then went into the back of his crate and promptly fell asleep.

"You look like you just lost your best friend." Cullen strode over to the kitchen sink, rolled up his sleeves and washed his arms up to the elbows.

She waited until he'd grabbed a towel and then moved in to wash up, too. "Not exactly," she murmured.

"Then what, exactly?"

She drew a deep breath. "My plan to be out of here— maybe as soon as this evening—fizzled. At least temporarily."

He kept his eyes locked with hers.

"The house I have put an offer on is currently empty. I was hoping the owners would allow me to rent it from them until I can close on the property. They told my Realtor, Jeanne Phipps, they would consider it, but only after all the inspections are done and my mortgage application is approved."

"How long do you think that will take?"

"Three, four weeks minimum. Which means I have to come up with a new plan to get us out of here."

"Maybe not," he corrected with a smile.

She regarded him quizzically.

"You could continue to stay here."

She pressed a hand against her trembling lips and drew a deep, bolstering breath. "After what happened last night?"

He leaned close enough for her to inhale the brisk fragrance of sun and man. "What happened last night?"

She gave him a droll look. He gave her one back.

Ignoring the warmth of his body so close to hers, she reminded wryly, "You kissed me."

His mouth quirked in masculine satisfaction. "And you kissed me back."

Boy, had she ever. In fact, she had spent the night dreaming about it. She scowled in renewed embarrassment. "We can't do that."

He threw his arm around her shoulders and gave them a companionable hug. "Why not?"

Tingling everywhere he touched and everywhere he didn't, she averted her glance. "My life is complicated enough as it is."

He tucked a hand beneath her chin and guided her face back to his. "News flash, Bridgett. It's always going to be complicated." His deep voice sent another thrill soaring through her. "That doesn't mean you can't enjoy yourself."

"Is that what we were doing?" Her throat was thick with

emotion. "Simply enjoying ourselves?" Because to her it felt as if they had been on the brink of much, much more.

He brushed his thumb across her cheek, then dropped his hand at the sound of a car coming up the drive. He went to window, looked out. Swore.

Her pulse jumped again. "Who is it?"

"My folks." He grimaced.

"Want me to make myself scarce?"

He caught her wrist before she could escape. "Nope. There's a chance—a remote one—your being here will help them censor their remarks."

"If I didn't know better, I'd think you were scared of them, Cullen Reid McCabe."

He shoved his hands through his hair. "In awe, maybe. And you'd be damned right." He swung open the front door before they had a chance to ring the bell and wake the little ones. "Hey. Frank. Rachel. You-all know Bridgett?"

As always, the handsome couple radiated warmth and good cheer. The petite blonde Rachel smiled. In a cardigan set, skirt and heels, a strand of pearls around her neck, she looked as if she had come straight from her work as a tax attorney. Frank's jeans, shirt and vest indicated he had left his work on the ranch. "Actually, we know her entire family," Rachel said. A long, awkward pause followed.

Cullen nodded at the picnic hamper in his dad's hand and the long wicker basket stuffed with baby things in his stepmother's. "What do you have there?"

"We heard about what happened," Rachel said gently, "and we brought by some dinner and a few baby items to help out in the interim."

It was a nice gesture. Or would have been, Bridgett thought, if Cullen obviously didn't resent the interference.

Frank frowned as Cullen ushered them inside. "We

were disappointed you didn't call us to tell us about the situation yourself."

With a sober nod, he relieved his father of the basket of food and carried it back to the kitchen. "How'd you hear?"

His dad glanced into the family room where baby and puppy were sleeping. "I think the question is who *didn't* call to let us know about the note left with the baby."

Ouch, Bridgett thought as she took the Moses basket from Rachel with a grateful smile.

"Can we see the baby?" Rachel asked eagerly.

Cullen tensed. "If you promise not to wake either of them."

Who was sounding like a daddy now? Bridgett wondered.

Everyone tiptoed toward the baby carrier.

Robby was sound asleep. He'd worked one arm out of the swaddling—it rested on the center of his chest. A blue knit cap covered most of his dark curly hair. His cheeks were slightly pink, his bow-shaped lips pursed. He was the epitome of sweetness and innocence.

On the floor opposite the Pack 'n Play, Riot was curled up in his crate, eyes closed, chin resting on a stuffed toy. He, too, was slumbering away.

"Adorable," Rachel whispered approvingly.

For Frank, the emotions seemed more complex.

They trooped back out of the family room. Cullen grabbed four bottles of sparkling water from the fridge and ushered everyone out onto the screened-in back porch, leaving the door to the kitchen open so they could hear.

Everyone sat.

He waited.

"I'm just going to be blunt," Frank said, looking at his eldest son. "Rachel and I both understand why you might have felt awkward about coming to us with this.

It had to have been a shock, finding out about Robby the way you did. But surely you'd know that I would understand, better than anyone, what it's like to get news like this after the fact."

Cullen held up a staying hand. "Before you continue, you both should know, he's not mine."

Frank and Rachel exchanged concerned looks.

Finally, his stepmom cleared her throat and said kindly, "What we're trying to tell you, Cullen, is that it would be okay, if he was. A McCabe is a McCabe. Part of our family, no matter how they come into it. Whether it's by marriage."

"Or illegitimacy?" Cullen challenged.

Frank leveled Cullen with a disappointed look.

Silence fell once again, more awkward and fraught with emotion than ever.

Finally, Cullen bit out, "Have you talked to Dan?"

Frank nodded. "He said attempts are being made to find the mother, but without her DNA, the child's true parentage may never be known. And that would be a shame, son. For everyone."

His words hung in the air, simultaneously an indictment and a plea to come clean.

Uncomfortable, Bridgett rose. "I really don't think I should be here for this."

Cullen put a hand on her shoulder. "This concerns you, too."

Not wanting to contribute to what increasingly felt like an emotional melee, Bridgett eased back into the chair.

Cullen turned back to Frank and Rachel. "I am not dissembling when I tell you and everyone else the child could not possibly be mine. Obviously, I've been tapped to be the responsible party. Why, I have no clue. *Yet.* But

I will figure this out. And when I do—" he turned back to his parents and finished heavily "—you-all will be the first to know."

"ARE YOU OKAY?" Bridgett asked, short minutes later, after his father and stepmother had left.

His broad shoulders flexed against the soft chambray of his shirt. Exasperation colored his low tone, resentment his eyes. "What do you think?"

Knowing that he needed her support, whether he realized it or not, she ignored his curt reply. "You really don't have any idea who did this, do you?"

An awkward silence fell. "You're *just now* figuring this out?"

Hating the fact he thought she had betrayed him in some way, she gave in to impulse and caught his arm before he could turn away. "I can see why the accusation—never mind an anonymous one—would be upsetting, Cullen." The hard curve of his biceps warmed beneath her fingertips. "But I can also see it goes much deeper than that."

He didn't take his eyes off her. "Let me guess," he muttered. "You want to talk about my illegitimacy, too."

She blinked, taken aback. Dropped her grasp and moved away. "Were you born illegitimately?"

"You don't know?"

"How would I?" When he'd been a junior in high school, she'd been in sixth grade. Way too young to hear that kind of talk.

His dark brow furrowed. "I thought everyone in the county knew."

"Obviously they don't," she returned, equally blunt, "or I would have heard about it."

A skeptical silence fell.

She folded her arms in front of her. "All I do know is that you're Frank's son, conceived several years before he married Rachel, and you came to live with him after your mother died when you were a teenager. That you were here for almost two years, went off to college, lived elsewhere for most of the last decade and then came back."

His eyes held hers for a long, discomfiting moment.

Ignoring the fluttering in her middle, she trod even closer. "I had no idea your mother and father were not married when you were born, but really, Cullen, in this day and age, is that such a big deal?" After all, she was attempting to adopt as a single parent! There were plenty of families where the parents were divorced, too.

Jaw set, he spun away and strode toward the front of the house where his office was. "It is a huge deal, even in this day and age to have 'unknown father' on your birth certificate."

Okay, she thought, reeling at the implications. Maybe that was a little different. She watched him check the security screens, find nothing amiss. "Are you saying your mom didn't *know* who sired you?"

Cullen dropped down into his desk chair, deep frown lines bracketing his mouth. "No. She knew. She just didn't want anyone else to know that she had a child by one of the Texas McCabes."

Bridgett leaned against the front of his desk, facing him, and took a moment to absorb that. Her denim-clad thigh almost touching his, she peered at him closely. "So, what *did* she tell you then?"

He rocked back in his chair, long legs stretched out in front of him, looking sexy as all get-out. "Nothing— except that it wasn't important who my biological father was. She was parent enough."

"And that was a problem because…?"

"She refused to accept the shame in the continued public perception that she 'had no idea' who her baby daddy was, and instead, cast herself as the lead in some romantic, ongoing stage play of life." He shook his head in obvious regret. "Raising me on her own was all part of the drama and the angst."

"She made you feel like a burden?"

"It wasn't her intention. But it was definitely the outcome." His expression didn't change in the slightest, yet there was something in his eyes. Some small glimmer of sorrow. "My mother worked as a ranch-house chef. She never had a problem getting jobs, because she was very talented. But she never stayed in one more than a year or so, because by then her romance of the moment would have fizzled out, and she would need a fresh start and move on."

Bridgett began to see how this had all played out for Cullen. "Taking you with her."

He gave a terse nod. "To another small, rural town, often in yet another state, where I would again have to register for school." His lips thinned in frustrated remembrance. "And to do that, I would have to provide my formal birth certificate. The administrators would see I had 'no known father.' My mother would tackle the subject head-on. Treat it as a joke and wear it as a badge of honor."

Gently, Bridgett said, "That must have been difficult for you to deal with at such a young age."

Cullen accepted her empathy with a downward slant of his mouth and a harsh exhalation of breath. "Pity was the most common reaction." He shook his head sadly, recalling, "I just felt embarrassed and degraded. To the point I begged my mother to tell me the truth."

The pain in his eyes matched his voice.

"I wanted her to get the name on the birth certificate

and be done with it. I even promised her I would never contact my father." He walked to the windows overlooking the front of the house, then paced to another window, another view. "I just didn't want to go through the rest of my life wondering who I was, where I came from. But—" he spun around and flung out a hand "—she wouldn't budge."

Bridgett's heart broke for him. Yet she had to ask, as she edged closer yet again. "Is it possible she really didn't know?"

Cullen shook his head, certain. "No. She was very much a one-man woman for as long as she was with someone. That was part of her own moral code. And, besides, I knew her. I could see that she knew my father's identity. She just wasn't going to tell me."

Bridgett stood opposite him, her shoulder braced against the window. She hadn't expected him to reveal this much about himself. Now that he had, it had opened up the floodgates of emotion within her, too. "Then how did you end up with Frank?" she asked curiously.

"My mom died in a car accident when I was fifteen. I was put in foster care for about a year, which was a horrendous experience, mostly because I was so angry about the fact that now I was never going to know who my dad really was or have the chance to meet him."

He exhaled. "Luckily, I had a social worker who understood how torn up I was about that, so she got a detective on the local police force to help. He used my birth records and my mother's work history to figure out where she had been employed when I was conceived." He grimaced. "From there, he found out she'd had a romantic relationship with Frank McCabe that lasted almost a year."

She studied the sober lines of his handsome face. Thought about the hell he'd been put through, not just after he'd been orphaned, but throughout his entire childhood.

"Frank apparently wanted to get married. Mom didn't, so they broke up, and she took off for parts unknown."

She listened empathetically, unsure how to help. Cullen's eyes took on a stormy hue. "A couple years after that, Frank married Rachel and no one ever gave my mom another thought. Until the social worker told Frank her suspicions."

"How did you verify it?"

"I had some belongings of my mom's. A hairbrush still had some of her hair in it. So they used that and Frank's DNA to determine I was their child." His manner guarded, he continued, "Frank immediately brought me to Texas. Rachel welcomed me as part of the family. And so did my five half siblings."

She shot him a commiserating look, guessing, "No one in Laramie made you feel demeaned…?"

"Of course not." He straightened and moved away from the window. "I was part of the legendary Texas McCabes. But they wouldn't have, even if I hadn't been from a well-known Texas family," he said gruffly. "Laramie isn't that kind of place."

"No. It's not." It was why she loved it so.

"Here, it's all about neighbor helping neighbor," he continued. "Everyone feeling like family, even if there isn't an actual biological connection."

"That's why I'll never leave here. Because it was that kind of community support after my own parents died when I was in middle school that helped me move on." He nodded and she touched his arm gently, feeling the kinship between them grow. "Is that why you came back to Laramie County? Because you wanted to live in a warm and welcoming place again?"

Was he perhaps more sentimental and idealistic than

he wanted to admit? Was it possible they could connect on that level, too? Because if so...

Unfortunately, he hesitated just a second too long for comfort. Finally, he said, "My family all wanted me here."

Bridgett's heart sank as she read the reluctance in his expression. "But *you* didn't really *want* to come back home, did you?"

CULLEN WASN'T SURE how to answer that. Not in a way a woman like Bridgett would understand, anyway. Finally, he said, "I hoped being with my dad and his family—as an adult, this time—would give me the kind of peace I've never had. Instead, it just feels like I'm waiting for the other shoe to drop. Something to happen. Some evidence that I am just as much my heartless, irresponsible, overly sentimental mom as I am my strong, hardworking, responsible father."

Bridgett let out a slow breath, the warm understanding in her eyes a balm to his soul. "And now it's happened. With this baby and this puppy."

Keeping his gaze meshed with hers, he confided ruefully, "On the surface, at least to other people, including Frank and Rachel and the rest of the McCabes, it would certainly seem so." He leaned in closer. "Which is why I have to find out who Robby's real parents are. Otherwise..."

Bridgett stared at him unhappily. "I'll convince DCFS that I'm the right mom for Robby and Riot, and foster-adopt them and they'll both be loved and cared for and have an amazingly happy life?"

He regretted the angry flush in her cheeks. "I know it hurts you to hear this." He captured her wrist before she could turn away. "But it's true. Robby will never be as happy as he could be unless the mystery is solved and he knows who he is, what his past is and why his mother or father—or whoever it was—left him and Riot at the fire station to be given into my care." He gave a ragged sigh. "And you won't be happy, either, if you and Robby and Riot have to live the way I have all my life, just waiting for the truth to finally come along and blow your life to smithereens."

Her silky skin warmed beneath his touch. She pulled away and threw up her hands in frustration. "But if that happens, Cullen, and you do find out who surrendered him so heartlessly and irresponsibly, I could end up losing Robby and Riot forever."

"Or end up keeping them forever," he pointed out sagely, looking deep into her eyes. "Either way, Bridgett, for all our sakes, we have to do whatever it takes to discover the truth."

Chapter Five

"The Monroe family wants to do something for you-all. We're just not sure what's appropriate," Bridgett's older sister, Erin, said later that evening.

Bridgett pushed the speaker button on her cell phone. With Cullen out on the ranch, prepping the Western Cross barns for the upcoming video tour in advance of the virtual cattle auction, and Robby and Riot both snoozing peacefully in the next room, she was free to talk to the closest thing she had to a mom these days.

"I know. And I appreciate it." If she'd come by a baby the traditional way, there would have been showers and parties galore to celebrate.

"I'm mailing some of my boys' old newborn clothing, and a few toys. Plus a few new things. Sleepers, T-shirts, booties, knit caps."

Tears blurred Bridgett's eyes. "Thank you," she managed. "It will really help."

Gently, Erin continued, "Mac and I were surprised not to see anything about the foundling on the news."

Bridgett saw Cullen's pickup truck coming down the lane toward the ranch house. She turned away from the window, relaying what she had initially been stunned to learn, too. "The authorities don't publicly announce any infants turned over via the Texas Safe Haven law. The assurance of privacy—for both baby and parent—is what keeps the program going." And little ones who might not otherwise be well cared for, safe.

"So, when will they know if the child has any other family willing to claim him?"

Bridgett's heart twisted in her chest at the thought of losing the little boy she was quickly coming to think of as her very own. "I'm not sure." She explained everything currently being done, the lack of results thus far.

Erin paused. "How long do you get to foster Robby?"

Bridgett tensed at the worry in her sibling's voice. "Another twelve days, until the DCFS makes its recommendation to the court."

"Well, if you need any character references…"

"I'm hoping my care will speak volumes. And make me the exception to the rule." Bridgett looked up to see Cullen standing in the portal. They hadn't parted well after their last discussion. She had to get her thoughts in order.

Struggling not to notice how good he looked with the blue chambray of his shirt bringing out the deep navy of his eyes, she fastened her gaze on the strong column of his throat and the tufts of curly espresso-colored hair visible in the open collar of his shirt.

When she felt composed enough, she returned her glance to his. His eyes lit up in the way they always did when he wanted her full attention and knew he had it.

Aware they had to find a way to make peace, even when they didn't agree on something, she flashed him a brisk, businesslike smile and said, "Listen, Erin, I have to go…"

CULLEN HADN'T KNOWN what kind of reception he would get upon returning to the ranch house. Bridgett hadn't exactly been happy with him when he'd left. But there was no helping it. He'd had to be honest with her about his intention of doing everything possible to discover Robby and Riot's real family. Even as Bridgett worked to keep them with her.

Fortunately, that was a bridge they didn't need to cross quite yet. It was enough right now to take things as they had been, an hour or two or three at a time.

He went to the sink to wash up. "Sara Anderson called. She's going to be over tomorrow to certify the health of the herd for the virtual auction. She suggested she do the puppy physical at the same time."

Finished, he grabbed a towel and turned back to her, noting how pretty Bridgett looked in a buttercup-yellow Western shirt and jeans. "I wasn't sure if you'd want to be there…"

Bridgett lit up at the mention of the puppy they had both quickly come to adore. "I do."

"It'll be later in the day. Not sure exactly what time." Kneeling down to the cushion where Riot dozed, he smiled at the pup's sleepy-eyed glance and affectionately patted his head. Then he moved to the Moses basket on the sofa table where the swaddled newborn slept, while Bridgett went about measuring powdered formula into the bottles she had lined up on the countertop.

"How was Riot this evening?" he asked casually, savoring the sweet intimacy of the situation.

She slanted him a contented smile. "I don't know what the two of you did when you were out on the ranch today, but he's pooped." She moved down the line, adding filtered water as she went. "He slept the entire time you were gone."

"Good." Cullen nodded, and inched closer to the slumbering child. Touching Robby's cheek with the back of his hand, he felt the fragile warmth of his skin.

He watched as Bridgett finished and put the baby bottles into the fridge.

He remembered kissing her, right here, right about this time, the evening before. Knew he had to do something—*anything*—to distract himself. Not sure why this felt so much like a date that wasn't going particularly well, he said, "I'm guessing you already had dinner?"

She wiped down the counters where she had been working, dropped the disposable cleaning cloth into the trash. "Around seven."

She was definitely the model of efficiency. Another thing they had in common. "How was it?"

She swung back to face him, her soft lips twisted into an aloof smile. "You're in for a treat. Rachel's chicken tortilla casserole was fantastic."

Could this get any more awkward?

"Rachel's a great cook." He took the containers his stepmother had brought over earlier out of the fridge. "She's always bringing food by for me and dropping it off." He spooned a generous amount onto his plate. "That's where last night's meatloaf dinner came from, too."

Bridgett moved to the other side of the island. Her slender hands folded in front of her, she perched on the edge of a stool. Drew a breath that raised and lowered the shapely lines of her breasts. "Sounds nice."

"Yeah. It is." He covered his plate with waxed paper and put it into the microwave to heat. "She says she's forgotten how to cook for fewer than a dozen people and has to do something with all the excess."

Bridgett twisted the length of her hair and put it back up into a clip. "Not buying it?"

Aware he liked her glossy dark brown hair up as much as down, he shrugged.

"I think she just likes an excuse to drop by and see her kids."

The corners of her luscious lips curved up. "You included."

Cullen nodded.

And if he stood here much longer, talking with her about the intimate details of his life while she looked so sexy and beautiful, he'd end up kissing her again. Still waiting on the microwave to finish, he opened the fridge and pulled out an icy-cold beer and the green salad.

In the Moses basket, Robbie began to fidget and fuss a little in his struggle to wake up. "I think I'll take him upstairs to feed him and get him ready for bed," she said.

He couldn't blame her for wanting an exit.

The situation between them was making him want family, too, and not just any family. And that couldn't be good for any of them, given how this was likely to end.

THE EVENING BEFORE, Bridgett had been cool to Cullen. The next morning, Cullen was polite but distant to her. And though the new caution with each other was probably wise, she still didn't like the way it felt. As if they were erecting artificial barriers around their hearts.

It couldn't be good for Riot and Robby, either. They seemed to sense the underlying tension between the two adults caring for them and were a little more fussy than usual. Not surprisingly, the little ones' cantankerous moods ended when the four of them split up for the day. Riot went off with Cullen, accompanying him on ranch work, while Robbie stayed at the ranch house with her.

Bridgett worried about what it would be like when they met up again, but luckily, at the end of the day, they had Sara Anderson's cheerful professional presence and the puppy's exam to distract them.

"Word around town is that little Riot here is a dead ringer for a stray you took in as a kid. Which is funny because I never knew you had a puppy *also called Riot* in the past," Sara Anderson said, lifting the new Riot onto the scale to weigh him.

Neither had Bridgett.

And even more curious…why hadn't Cullen mentioned this to her? He'd said he had one dog as a kid. He hadn't said that dog had been named Riot. And that was a pretty big deal, having a stray show up that was named after the dog he'd had in his youth.

Although he certainly did not owe her an explanation, deep down she felt a little betrayed he hadn't confided in her.

Cullen looked equally unhappy about the fact this part of the story was also now public knowledge. Frowning, he folded his arms and moved closer to the ongoing exam. "Who'd you hear that from?" he asked Sara.

The veterinarian listened to Riot's heart and lungs with a stethoscope. "I think it might have been my receptionist, who heard it from your little sister."

Cullen groaned. As well he might, Bridgett thought. Lulu McCabe was a chatterbox and then some.

"I don't know how Lulu'd know of any physical resemblance between the two," Cullen muttered.

Bridgett tilted her head, perplexed.

He frowned. "I never showed the photos of my late dog to anyone here."

"But your entire family knew about the pet," Bridgett ascertained.

He nodded.

"What did Riot Senior look like?" Bridgett asked.

"He was a black, brown and white German shepherd, chocolate Lab, collie mix."

"So, in reality there isn't much physical similarity between the two Riots, aside from the color of their coats," Bridgett surmised, wondering what the connection was.

"Correct, since Riot Junior appears to be all beagle and golden retriever," Sara remarked as she examined his eyes, ears and nose.

Cullen raised his brows. "How can you tell?"

Sara looked at the mutt's mouth and teeth. "The shape of his face and eyes, the long snout. The floppy ears. Silky coat and tail…"

Bridgett sighed dreamily. "He is cute."

"Definitely," Sara agreed, palpating the puppy's abdomen and lymph nodes.

"And very sweet," Bridgett continued. Hearing Robby fuss, she went to get him.

"Maybe the two of you should start a fan club," Cullen teased.

"Or a new breed," Sara Anderson suggested, grinning as Bridgett rejoined them. "One that will win Grand Champion at the dog shows every time."

United by the puppy, they all smiled.

"Why haven't you ever mentioned you like dogs?" Sara asked Cullen.

He watched her give the vaccinations. "It wasn't a big deal. I like all animals."

Except it was a big deal, given how quickly he had bonded with the mutt, Bridgett thought. As quickly as she had bonded with Robby.

"Well, all I can say is that this one seemed attached to your hip when you strode up here. How many days has it been now?" Sara prodded.

Shrugging, Cullen replied, "Three and a half days."

Three and a half days that were changing their lives, Bridgett thought.

Three and a half days to tell her how much she knew about the Cullen behind the mask of gruff chivalry and how much she didn't.

"How old is the puppy?" Bridgett asked.

Sara made a few notes on the chart. "He still has all his baby teeth, so I'm guessing around twelve weeks. Do you want to microchip in case he gets lost again?"

"*Yes*," Bridgett and Cullen said, unexpectedly in unison.

Sara smiled at them. "Okay, that can be done in the office if you schedule an appointment. In the meantime, you're going to want to get some tags on him. Or a collar with his contact information."

"I've already ordered both," Cullen said, stunning Bridgett yet again. "They should be delivered in the next day or so. What?" He mugged at their astonished looks. "I'm efficient."

Sara smiled tenderly at the little mutt and scratched him behind the ears. "Well, I hope you get to keep him—if he doesn't already have a family, and I'm guessing not, or we would have seen posters up for him as well as calls to the shelters in the last week. The Fire Department faxed his photo around, too. In any case, I think you should get a dog for yourself, McCabe. Better yet—" Sara winked "—you can train one of my therapy dogs."

Culled squinted. "I thought those were only for military vets."

"Not all of our wounded warriors can train their own companion dogs. Some need their service animals trained for them. Which is where you would come in."

Cullen promised readily. "I'll see what I can do to help out with that, after the auction."

"Good. Bridgett, nice to see you again. We need to

spend more time together. Catch up. Get to know each other all over again. High school was a loooong time ago."

Bridgett laughed. "No kidding."

Vet bag in hand, Sara headed for the door.

When they were alone again, Bridgett turned to Cullen. "Why didn't you tell me both dogs were named Riot?"

CULLEN HAD FIGURED she wouldn't be happy about the oversight. "I was hoping to figure out what the link was, first."

"And have you?"

He worked to contain his frustration. "No. But when I eventually do, I promise you'll be the first to know."

To his surprise, Bridgett looked appeased.

Infant in her arms, she walked with him out into the yard, standing nearby while the leashed Riot did what he had to do. She turned to him, her eyes full of questions. "I'd really like to see some photos of the original Riot."

The last time he'd reminisced over his deceased family pet, it had stirred up a grief that nagged at him for days. "I'm not really sure where they are," Cullen fibbed.

"If you come across any, then…"

He nodded, promising nothing. Together, they walked inside the ranch house. Turning her attention back to the baby in her arms, she said, "Hey, little fella, you have one damp diaper." She put him down on the changing pad atop the sofa, unsnapped his sleeper and opened up the soiled diaper.

Cullen winced at the ugly yellow stump emerging from the center of Robby's little tummy. "Is he okay?" he asked in alarm.

Bridgett cleaned the area gently. "This is the umbilical cord."

"Is it supposed to look like that?"

Her nursing background coming into play, Bridgett sent

him a reassuring glance. "Yes. It takes ten days to three weeks for it to heal completely and fall off. And just so you're prepared—during that time it will go from yellow to brown to black."

He exhaled, still watching intently, still keeping his distance. "You know, this could be a problem. How little you know about babies and how little I know about dogs."

He settled Riot on his dog cushion and watched her put a fresh diaper on Robby. "What are you suggesting?"

"That we switch for a while."

Cullen would have thought she was joking, save for the serious look on her face as she finished dressing Robby and then put him in his Moses basket. "How about you give him a bottle and rock him for a while, and I'll take Riot for a walk."

"Why would we want to do that when this is all working so well?"

Her chin jerked up. "Because we're living on a ranch miles from town, and you're my backup with Robby and I'm yours with Riot."

"Exactly. Backup." His gaze moved over her silky-soft lips before returning to focus on the tumult in her pretty green eyes. "The likelihood of either of us needing to do the other's job is almost nil."

"*Almost* being the operative word." She looked at him for a long, quelling moment then propped her hands on her hips. "Look, I didn't mention it, because I thought I would be long gone by now, but, because the three of us—" she made a sweeping motion with one hand "—are staying here at your very kind invitation, I'm *forced* to make a case to social services that this situation *really is* best for the baby. Plus, you said you wanted to be responsible."

He caught the hint of accusation in her low tone. Wishing he could kiss her again, without fear of driving her away, he retorted equally, "And I do."

"So?" she challenged with a tilt of her pretty head. "What's the big deal, then?"

He was competent on the ranch, in the kitchen and the bedroom, but this…spending time with her and the baby… threw him for a loop. She was still staring at him like he was the most perplexing person on Earth.

He exhaled and said matter-of-factly, "The big deal is I don't know anything about babies, never mind an infant that was just born a few days ago."

Bridgett adapted a defiant stance. "Actually, Robby is at least a week old now. So far as we can tell, anyway."

For a moment, they both fell silent again. Cullen tried not to be bummed about the fact that they might never know specifically where or when Robby had been born. He thought it had been tough growing up without a named dad. Not having knowledge of *either* parent would really leave a kid rudderless.

His protective instincts escalated. "He's still way too young to be left alone with a novice."

She wrinkled her nose. "You might have a point."

"I always have a point."

She laughed softly. "Okay." She tried again. "How about I heat the bottle and then we sit together on the porch swing. You can feed Robby while I talk you through it, and then we'll take everyone on a walk. You can push the convertible stroller, and I'll handle the leash, and you can instruct me on the proper way to do that." She flashed him a wry smile. "So I'm not being dragged along the way I have every time I've tried to take Riot somewhere by myself."

It was a reasonable request. One, in the end, he couldn't refuse.

ALTHOUGH BRIDGETT HAD TAUGHT a lot of new moms and dads how to handle a newborn baby, she hadn't ever instructed someone she was attracted to. However, she sort of liked the idea of Cullen turning to her, even if it was just for information.

Sitting close enough to him to be able to reach out and help, if needed, she inhaled the brisk masculine scent of his hair and skin as she watched Cullen gingerly hold Robby in both his big hands.

"Support his head and neck." She put her hands beneath Cullen's, to help guide him, trying not to notice how strong and masculine he felt. "Snuggle Robby in one arm and cradle him against your chest. Keep his head a little higher than his body. Yes, like that." Her pulse racing, she handed over the bottle of warmed formula. "Now, offer the bottle. When he feels the nipple against his lips he'll know what to do."

She flushed at the unintended double entendre. Shook her head. "Sorry. That was…"

Successfully following her instructions, Cullen said, "True?" Mischief glimmered in his eyes. So he was feeling the sexual awareness, too!

His flirtatious gibe sent a shiver of awareness spiraling through her. It was a good thing they were well chaperoned. Otherwise, who knew what might happen between them? She pretended an aloofness she couldn't begin to feel. "Ha, ha."

His sexy grin widened. "I aim to amuse and be helpful, too."

Which could be a problem, Bridgett thought, rolling her eyes. Since she already had been wondering what it might be like to kiss him just one more time. Luckily, they had tasks ahead of them that would prevent just that from happening.

"So, what next?" Cullen asked, as Robby drank hungrily.

Exactly what you think. We proceed, oh, so cautiously. And try not to kiss again—never mind be tempted to recklessly make love!

Tamping down her rising desire, Bridgett turned her full attention back to the baby, then continued in the soft, encouraging tone she used with all new parents. "You're going to want to feed him an ounce. Two at most, then stop and burp him, so he doesn't get too much air in his tummy."

Cullen watched the baby feed with a surprising air of contentment. "We wouldn't want that," he cooed softly, smiling as Robby tapped his hand against the side of the bottle.

"No," Bridgett agreed, acutely aware of what a good daddy Cullen would make. Even if he didn't yet know it. "We wouldn't…"

For another minute or so, they sat in silence. Savoring the wonder of the moment, the peace that could be had when caring for new life. Was this what it would be like if they had been Robby's parents? All Bridgett knew for certain was that something about this whole situation was more magical and alluring than anything she had ever felt before.

Cullen seemed introspective, too.

Finally, he took the bottle away, checked and saw that about an ounce and a half of formula had been ingested. He handed her the bottle, then shifted Robby upright against his shoulder, in the same way she knew he had seen her do.

The sight of the big, strapping cowboy holding the fragile infant with so much awkward tenderness was almost her undoing. Again, she talked Cullen through the basics of burping. He patted Robby's back gently until a resounding belch filled the air.

Cullen chuckled, impressed by the man-size effort. "Do I feed him again?"

"Yes."

He shifted Robby with a little more confidence this time, nestled him in his strong arm and held him against his chest.

"Know what to do?"

"Feed. Burp. Repeat."

"You've got it, cowboy." Bridgett eased away from him, realizing she had been sitting way too close on the swing.

Her heart swelling with all she was feeling, she watched as a big silver pickup truck came up the lane. "Are you expecting someone?"

"No. You?"

Bridgett shook her head. The luxury vehicle came to a halt, and the local Cattleman's Association president stepped out. Bridgett half expected Cullen to shift the baby to her arms. Instead, he nodded at their guest. "Let him know we're back here," he said.

Bridgett stepped off the screened-in porch. "Hey, Sam!" she called to one of the biggest supporters of the hospital fund-raiser every year.

Kirkland waved and strode toward them. His glance cut to Cullen, who still didn't let go of the baby. He held his hat against his chest. "Hope this isn't a bad time."

Seeing Robby had taken another ounce of formula, Cullen shifted him to his shoulder to burp. "What's up?"

"I'm just checking to see if there's anything the association can do to support your upcoming virtual auction."

Cullen used the corner of the burp cloth to dab at the milk bubbles appearing on the corners of Robby's lips.

"Vouch for the quality of my breeding program if anyone asks."

Sam cut a glance toward Bridgett. Cullen gave the other rancher a look indicating he should continue.

"Actually, we already have had a number of calls the past few days, with questions about your cattle operation," Sam said.

Cullen frowned. "Which doesn't usually happen."

Sam grimaced. "Not to someone of your reputation who is auctioning off purebred Hotlander cattle, no."

A tense silence fell. Cullen exhaled heavily, even as he kept right on feeding Robby. "It's about the baby and the puppy…"

Sam cleared his throat. "Well…you know. People talk. And character counts."

Cullen squinted at their guest. "And people wonder why I'm still denying what they feel is obvious?"

Sam Kirkland sidestepped that landmine. "Look, all I'm saying is that if you want to delay your sale until things settle down, no one would fault you for it."

"No." Cullen stood, gently handing Robby to Bridgett then squaring off with their guest. "I've got nothing to hide. Nothing to feel ashamed about. And I'll be damned if I'm going to act like I do."

Chapter Six

"You're sure you still want to go on a walk?" Bridgett asked short minutes later, after a drowsy and content Robby had been strapped into his convertible stroller.

Cullen snapped the leash onto Riot's collar. "That was our deal." He flexed his brawny shoulders, the motion as careless as his attitude. "You teach me. I teach you…"

"But after what just happened. With Sam Kirkland…"

He shrugged, as if the inquiries into his trustworthiness were of no consequence. "It's a nice afternoon for a walk and everyone is cooperating."

"Well, maybe it will help dissipate the steam coming out of your ears."

To her frustration, he didn't even crack a smile. He was back to being the grim, testy rancher who had come striding toward her in the hospital. He inhaled a long breath that expanded the impressive musculature of his chest and drew her attention to his washboard abs. "I know you mean well, Bridgett, but you don't need to be concerned about me."

"Really?" She toed off her flats, sat to slip on some boot socks then stretched out one leg at a time to pull on her favorite peacock-blue cowgirl boots. "Because you sure look like you need some emotional support."

Something flickered in his expression at that. Annoyance at having been thought to need anything or anyone, probably. "Is that what this is?" he asked in surprise.

Bridgett was suddenly stunned to realize how much she was beginning to care for him. "Isn't that what *you've* been giving *me* the past few days?"

His glance lingered on the bare skin of her upper calves between the boots and the hem of her denim skirt before moving over her fitted shirt to her face. He escorted the puppy to the other side of the threshold, then held the door for her. She gently pushed the stroller out.

Showered but unshaved, wearing a dark green canvas shirt and jeans, he was every inch the indomitable Texan. He sent her a level look, showing her how to situate Riot at her left side and hold the leash with two hands across her body. "I hadn't really thought about it."

Their fingertips brushed as he released her.

"Well, I have." Determined to get through to him, she ignored the new heat in her skin and said in a cajoling voice, "I think we could be friends, Cullen McCabe. Good ones."

"Friends," Cullen repeated. He came closer, his expression that of a lion stalking his prey.

Her heart did a funny little twist inside her chest. Needing a little space to compose herself, she moved herself and Riot to the other side of the stroller. "You don't want to be friends?"

Pushing the stroller down the long paved road that wound through the ranch, he gave her another sidelong glance. His expression didn't change in the slightest. Yet there was something, a small glimmer of bemusement, in his blue eyes. "Platonic friends?"

She fought a blush. Duh. "What other kind is there?"

He gave her a seductive look. "Come on. Don't act like

you're that surprised something more might be in our future. You felt that kiss as much as I did, the other night."

"So we have chemistry! It doesn't mean we have to act on it."

He slowed his pace to better accommodate hers. "Doesn't mean we can't, either." He gave her the sensual once over, his gaze returning to linger on her lips.

Wishing she didn't want to kiss him as much as she did, Bridgett huffed responsibly. "Am I going to be fending you off?"

Chuckling mischievously, he shot right back at her. "Am I going to be fending *you* off?"

She couldn't help it, his tone was so playful, she laughed. "How did we even get on this subject?" she drawled, her voice every bit as exasperated as his had been.

The warm spring breeze wafted through their hair and blew across their bodies. He put a hand around her waist and tugged her against him. Then he leaned over and whispered in her ear. "You were feeling me out on our... situation."

The unyielding imprint of his strong, hard body had her nipples tingling and pressing against her shirt. "Really?" she groaned, but she didn't move away. "You had to use that term?"

He met her gaze, his eyes dark and heated. "Can't help it," he teased in a way that made all rational thinking cease. Releasing a soft exhalation of breath, he cupped her face and rubbed his thumb across her cheek before dropping to explore the shape of her lower lip. "I like seeing you all spunky and indignant." Reluctantly, he let her go as the four of them continued on their stroll. "It brings a real sparkle to your eyes."

She had the strong impression he had been about to

kiss her again and still might. "For someone who is un-sentimental, you can certainly be a handful." She lifted a warning finger. "And don't even think about going down that verbal path…"

He grinned. "Whatever the lady wants…" He made a motion as if he was zipping his lips, locking them tight and throwing away the key.

They walked some more in silence, enjoying the day, each other. With conversation momentarily halted, Riot pulled ahead. Grateful for the much-needed diversion, Bridgett concentrated on her task. As did Cullen.

"Try varying your pace a little." He reached over to show her exactly how much pressure to exert on the leash. "You want Riot to be following you, not the other way around." He watched with masculine satisfaction as she did it on her own. A mixture of pleasure and unmet need rolled through her.

"That's it. Yeah. Nice."

She could imagine him giving her the same low, deep-throated encouragement in bed.

Cautioning herself not to wear her heart on her sleeve, she slanted him a look and broke the tension with a joke. "Are you talking to me or the dog?"

He waggled his brows. "Both."

Bridgett had never imagined he could be so playful. He was always so serious and businesslike. At least, around her. She wondered what else about him she had yet to see. "So, how come you're not married?" She blurted the first question that came to mind.

He slanted her a reluctant look. She wasn't surprised he didn't want to answer. Still, she pushed on. "You already know all about my romantic past." How she had given up her one shot at love and marriage and family. "What's your story, cowboy?"

"I'm single."

"Have you ever been married?"

He looked out at the pastures with a brooding expression. "Nope."

"Engaged?"

He bent to adjust the canopy around the still-sleeping Robby. "I was close a couple of years ago."

This hurt. Why, she couldn't say. "What happened?"

He continued grimly. "I brought her home for a weekend to meet my family."

The suspense was killing Bridgett. "And?"

His hands tightened on the handle. "She found out I was only half McCabe."

It was all Bridgett could do to keep walking. "So…?"

He finally turned to look at her. Their glances locked and they shared another moment of tingling awareness, an emotional connection Bridgett did not expect. "Theresa found that concerning. She thought that might affect my future inheritance."

Bridgett blinked. "She really said that?"

"She really did," Cullen reflected sadly. "Anyway, her interest in me cooled really quickly after that, but she was very interested in getting to know a couple of my brothers, so…when we got back to Oklahoma, I told her I didn't stand to inherit anything from Frank."

"Is that true?" It didn't sound like the McCabes she knew!

"No, but not too long after that she asked to start dating other people."

Because there were not going to be any large sums of money. *Nice.* Curious, Bridgett studied the rugged lines of his handsome profile. "*Did* she go after your brothers?"

Cullen smirked. If he was still heartbroken, Bridgett noted, he wasn't showing it. "Apparently she sent some pretty friendly private messages via social media. I'm not sure what my brothers said to her."

Hopefully they'd told her to take a hike!

"All I know is she has been incommunicado with my family and out of my life."

He appeared relieved. Bridgett couldn't blame him. "And there's been no one serious since then?"

"That *was* true," he said very quietly, gazing into her eyes.

Bridgett took a bolstering breath and forced herself to hold his gaze with the same calm, quiet deliberation he was holding hers. "Until?" she asked, her heart doing cartwheels in her chest.

His smile slowly widened.

She had the gut feeling he was about to kiss her again. And she knew, wise or not, she was going to kiss him back. Or would have, had Riot not chosen that particular instant to give out a short little bark at something in front of them.

Turning to check on her charge, Bridgett gasped at the unfolding calamity.

"YOU SURE YOU'RE OKAY?" Cullen asked twenty minutes later, walking into the upstairs bathroom, first-aid kit in hand. "Riot really dragged you through the brush."

Bridgett placed her foot on the edge of the tub so she could better see the scrapes she was tending to. They covered her calves, knees and lower thighs. Being careful to keep the hem of her denim skirt modestly down, she addressed each jagged cut with a cotton ball dipped in a numbing cleanser/antiseptic. "Note, though, I did not let go of the leash!"

"No, you didn't." Cullen handed her the tube of antibiotic cream from the first-aid kit. "And your fierce grip on him kept Riot from landing his first wild game." He stepped back slightly to give her room to work. Arms folded across his chest, he lingered in the portal of the smallish, old-fashioned bathroom. "Though I'm not sure what he would have done had he caught that squirrel."

"Me, either." They both laughed.

Their eyes met, held. "Well, he's certainly tuckered out now," Bridgett said softly.

"He is."

She straightened, aware all over again how much taller he was. How smoking hot. It didn't matter what time of day or night, or how he was dressed, whenever she looked into his eyes, felt that fierce magnetic pull, she wanted him.

It was crazy.

It was real.

It was....destiny?

Oblivious to the lusty nature of her thoughts, he leaned closer. Reached up and plucked a leaf from her hair with the same smitten look she had seen other men give their wives in the maternity ward. Her hand went up automatically. "Do I have anything else in there?"

Another lift of his impossibly wide shoulders. He shook his head mutely, his gaze still locked on hers. Her pulse skittered. Awareness grew. "Cullen..."

"I know," he told her gently threading the fingers of both hands through her hair and lowering his head. He gazed at her as if she were the most desirable woman in the entire world. "I'm feeling it, too."

The next thing she knew, his lips were on hers. Her arms were around his neck. The kiss—if you could call it just a kiss!—was more incredible than the first had been. With a low moan of appreciation, she pushed all the way against him, drinking in the heat and masculine feel of his hard physique. Her knees went weak, her lips opened to the dizzying pressure of his. Their tongues tangled as surely as their hearts. The next thing she knew, he was dancing her backward to the room at the end of the hall that held his king-size bed.

All it would have taken was one hand pressed against the center of his chest. One hint of dissent. She could have put on the brakes.

She didn't.

The truth was, he was as much her fate as Robby and Riot. And she was his. This was all meant to be. And she was determined to enjoy every single moment of it.

"You smell so good." He buried his face in her hair.

Arousal swept through her, more potent than before.

She kissed his neck. "So do you. Like sunshine and spring…"

He chuckled softly then dropped a string of kisses down the nape of her neck, across her cheek, up her jaw, then hovered over her lips. Passion roared through her, fierce as a tornado, as he pressed her lower half to his. She surged against him, softness to hardness. He kissed her, even more amorously this time. She could feel the strong, steady thrumming of his heart, beating in rhythm with hers. Lower still, there was a tingling need.

She melted against him. And they kissed and kissed and kissed. Until there wasn't any place she would rather be. He was hot and powerful and male. And he wanted her as much as she wanted him.

ALTHOUGH HE'D KNOWN the time would come, Cullen hadn't expected to make love to Bridgett just yet. He had planned to get to know her, spend quality time with her. After solving the mystery of why the puppy and baby had been left to him.

But that was before she had looked at him with such tender devotion. She had been alone a long time, too. Yet he needed to know she was all in before they took this any further. He caught her face in his hands and searched her eyes. "You're sure?"

"Very."

His glance fell to the nipples protruding through her top. He unbuttoned her blouse, unfastened her bra. Found the curves, the tips, the valley in between her breasts until she shuddered in response.

"You're so damn beautiful," he rasped, kissing her again, desire exploding in liquid heat.

She unbuttoned his shirt and palmed the contours of his chest. Lower still, she unzipped his jeans. Her hand closed over him as he reached beneath her skirt and divested her of her panties. He shifted her against the bureau and slid a knee between her thighs. She moved her weight onto it, building the pleasure even as he determined to make their lovemaking last. His mouth slid over her neck, dragging against the skin, and he felt her erotic little shiver. She whimpered in frustration, her body straining all the more, before abruptly finding the release she'd clearly been wanting.

Her head fell to his shoulder. He held her until her shudders stopped then finished undressing her and moved her to the bed.

He found a condom, stripped down and joined her.

She slid her hands down his sides, to his hips. He grinned as she arched up to kiss him again. "Now, where were we...?" he murmured roughly.

Impatience glimmered in her pretty eyes. She nipped his shoulder. "I want you in me."

All too ready to oblige, he eased his hands beneath her.

Her muscles trembled, tensed, as he settled between her thighs, his hips nudging hers apart.

Her hands rubbed his shoulders, stroked against his chest. They kissed again, their bodies immersed in friction, in need, in sweet, all-encompassing heat. He couldn't get enough of her as he slowly, erotically slid home, and she rose up to meet him, answering each fierce, deliberate thrust and intoxicating kiss. Until there was no more holding back, for either of them. It was all hot, out-of-control kisses and reckless daring and want and need. Until finally satisfaction came. Roaring through them both. And they collapsed, spent and shaking, in the warm protective embrace of each other's arms.

BRIDGETT WASN'T SURE how long it took her to catch her breath after they finally rocketed into oblivion. She did know she'd never been made love to like that. Like she was the most precious woman on Earth.

She did know she'd loved it. Every steamy moment of it. And that left her feeling surprisingly unsettled.

She wasn't supposed to be having a romance here. She was supposed to be figuring out a way to prove she was the best—the only—mother for little Robby. She was supposed to be solving her housing situation fast so she could get out of here and regain her usual levelheadedness, gosh darn it.

Ignoring her first instinct—which was to stay here, wrapped in his arms—she pushed against his chest and murmured, "Um…Cullen?"

Sleepy-eyed, content, he lay back against the pillows. Sensing she wanted her physical space, he reluctantly folded his arms behind his head. "Yes…Bridgett?" he echoed in a low teasing tone that had her wanting to make love to him again.

She reached for her panties and slipped into them, then her bra. To her embarrassment, he was still watching, enjoying the show. "I don't think we should do this again."

To her frustration, he did not look the least bit surprised. Or offended. He grinned at her good-naturedly. "Okay, we can make love in your bed next time."

"That is not what I meant!"

He sighed, sat up and reached for his boxer briefs. "Yeah. I know," he grumbled.

Ignoring the reckless warmth spiraling through her, Bridgett pushed aside the desire and held her ground. "I have a lot to get straightened out here. I can't afford to be sidetracked by a passionate interlude!"

He nodded. Tugged on his jeans. Zipped up his fly. Fastened his belt. Serious now, he asked, "What can I do to help?"

By the time they were fully dressed, Robby was awake, ready for his next feeding. Needing a little time to compose herself, she stayed upstairs to change his diaper, while Cullen went down to heat another bottle in the electric warmer his stepmother had brought over for them.

He got the puppy out of his crate and fed him, too. Then he glanced at her cell phone, which was blinking. "Looks like you've got some messages. I'll finish burping Robby if you want to check on that."

Bridgett sent him a grateful glance. "Thanks." Maybe they could go back to being team players, after all.

She read her message. "Excuse me while I make a call. The bank is long closed. But the loan officer processing my mortgage application is a friend, so…maybe it's some good news."

Except, Bridgett swiftly found out, it wasn't.

"EVERYTHING OKAY?" CULLEN ASKED when she finally hung up.

Turbulent emotions tautened her pretty features. "The bank wants to know if I intend to take a maternity leave to care for Robby."

He followed her into the kitchen and watched as she poured herself a lemonade. "And obviously you do."

"I'm on vacation for the next couple of weeks, so I'm still getting paid. But if I can overcome the obstacles and get approved to foster-adopt Robby I am entitled to family leave for six months." In a low voice, she added, "Unfortunately, that's unpaid, and I can only qualify for the loan if I am working at the time the mortgage is processed."

He summed up her dilemma, "So you'd have to close on the property before your vacation is up."

"Which I've just been told is impossible."

"Or go back to work until you do." His heart went out to her. "Sounds like you're between a rock and a hard place."

She sipped her lemonade. "Yep."

Wishing he could help her in some way, he studied the sober set of her soft lips. "What are you going to do?"

She straightened defiantly. "Talk to my Realtor again and see if there is some way I can convince the sellers to rent to me for the next six months, until I can get approved and close the deal."

More determined than ever, she went off.

A flurry of phone calls followed over the next few hours. And by the time she finally hung up, for what appeared the last time, it was clear from her dejected expression that she was in worse straits than before.

His eyes asked the question.

"The sellers won't budge," she informed him miserably. "They are living in a hotel in their new city, and they can't buy their new house unless they close on their old one, so if I can't get approved our deal is off. They're willing to return half of my earnest money, but that is the best they can do."

He took her hand. "I'm sorry."

"So am I. It was a great house. It would have been perfect for the three of us."

Not, Cullen thought, as perfect as the Western Cross ranch, for the four of them. But sensing she did not want to hear that just now, especially since there was still no guarantee someone else wouldn't show up to claim the baby, he said, instead, "You could always try for a private loan via promissory note."

Bridgett shook her head. "I don't want to lean on my siblings."

"I'm not talking about your siblings." He waited until she looked at him. "I'm talking about me."

Chapter Seven

Bridgett stared at him, sure she couldn't have heard right.

"You want to loan me money."

Cullen reached up and stroked her cheek as tenderly as he'd made love to her. "You're good for it, darlin'. Or, if you prefer, I could buy the property outright, rent to you now, and you could purchase it from me later."

Aware her life had taken another surreal turn, she blinked, not sure whether she should be grateful or insulted. Mostly she was just stunned. "You're unbelievable, you know that?"

More to the point, how and when had she ever given him the impression that she was the type of woman who would depend on a man *monetarily*?

His gaze drifted over her face. "I don't see what is so shocking." Moving away, he rummaged around in the fridge and brought out a container of pizza dough and a bag of shredded mozzarella cheese. "You need a place of your own to live, if you're to have the best chance of being chosen to foster-adopt Robby. And right now you don't have one, except for this ranch, which you don't seem to think is going to be an acceptable home—in the minds of those making the decision, anyway."

She moved to the other side of the island, to give him

room to work. "It's not the ranch. It's the arrangement. What it might seem to imply."

He set the oven to preheat then rolled the dough out onto a baking sheet. "What goes on between you and me, Bridgett, is between you and me."

The walls around his heart were as impenetrable as ever, yet there was no mistaking the sexual undertone in his low voice. Disappointment lanced her heart. "You're saying there are strings attached?"

It was his turn to look surprised. Nixing the allegation with a shake of his head, he lightly touched her forearm. "No strings."

Thank heaven!

"I am saying I'd like to make love to you again." He paused to let his words sink in. "I'm not going to lie about that. And judging by the fireworks in the bedroom, I think you want the same thing."

She did. That was the hell of it. She worked to keep her tone nonchalant. "I also need to prove that I can stand on my own two feet. Take care of myself and a baby and a dog without relying on the kindness of family and friends to do so."

That hit a chord. He opened a jar of pizza sauce, and spread it over the dough. "My mom used to say the same."

Not surprised he was as adept in the kitchen as he was everywhere else, Bridgett set her elbow on the counter and rested her chin on her hand. "And?"

"It was never true. Everywhere we went, there were people who reached out to help." He sprinkled shredded mozzarella onto the pizza, then added sliced pepperoni and precooked sausage. "Other moms who watched me when I was sick, so she could still go to work. Cowboys who taught me to ride and rope and took me out on the ranch to work right alongside them when I was out of school."

Salivating, she watched him slide their dinner into the oven to bake. "Is that how you became interested in ranching?"

He grabbed two light beers and came to sit next to her. "I loved being outdoors. Working the land, caring for the cattle. Being my own man."

Their knees touched as he swung toward her. "As long as we're on the subject…" He flashed her a sexy grin. "How did you decide to become a nurse?"

"I've just always loved taking care of people. My twin sister, Bess, feels the same. Nursing was the one career that made sense."

He tapped the neck of her bottle with his. "You have a lot to offer a child, Bridgett. Riot, too. With Mitzy's help, the people in the department will see that."

"I hope so." She didn't know what she would do if she lost the opportunity to be Robby's mother.

THEY ATE A quick dinner together. Bridgett shooed him off while she did the dishes, since he had cooked. And Cullen spent the rest of the evening answering questions to potential buyers about the Hotlander cattle he was putting up for auction, both by phone and on email. By the time he was finished it was midnight. Robby and Riot had long ago been put to bed for the night, and Bridgett was in the guest room, door shut. He passed by, saw from the arc of yellow light coming out from under the door the lamp was still on. He wanted to ask if everything was okay, but aware of all she had been through and was still dealing with, forced himself to respect her privacy.

The rest of the night passed uneventfully. He tossed and turned for a while, wishing he'd taken her back to his room for another bout of hot lovemaking, but knew he was treading on dangerous territory. Finally, he drifted off into a restless sleep. He came downstairs at 6:00 a.m. the following morning. Bridgett was already up and dressed.

"Need me to do anything before I head out?" he asked, hoping she'd say yes.

She gave him a sweetly contented look that made him want to make love to her all over again. "No. Everyone's been fed, changed and/or taken outside."

Noting the scrapes on her legs looked better, he nodded at the Mason jar in her hand. "What are you eating?"

She licked the back of the spoon. "Overnight oatmeal."

He moved closer, inhaling her lavender lotion scent. "What?"

She smiled at him as if sharing space like this was the most natural thing in the world. "You mix it with milk and other stuff and let it set overnight in the fridge." She waved an airy hand. "I made extra, if you want to try it. One has bananas, yogurt and pecans. Another one has fresh peach, almonds and coconut. And there's a blueberry, raspberry and blackberry one, too. Take your pick."

"Where'd you learn to do this?"

Her eyes lit up as she savored another bite. "Nursing school. We were encouraged to eat healthy to keep going." She shifted slightly, so he could get into the fridge. "The classes, studying and long shifts left little time to cook. So Bess and I figured out how to do as much as possible ahead so we could grab something from the fridge and go."

He chose the one with the bananas and took a place standing next to her.

The cereal was creamy, crunchy and sweet. "It's good." He took another bite. "Almost like a breakfast dessert."

From his infant seat, Robby looked around with interest. Bridgett picked up her phone and, adjusting the seat so the light coming in from the windows was just right, took a couple of quick photos. He couldn't blame her. The kid was adorable.

Not to be outdone, Riot—who had been lounging on his dog cushion—came closer, his tail wagging. Bridgett knelt down and took some photos of him, too.

Without warning, she turned the cell's camera lens toward Cullen and popped off a few more of him eating breakfast. "What are you doing?"

"Gathering photos for Robby's baby book." She gestured to the island counter, showing him the embossed white leather album with Baby's First Year written in gold leaf across the front.

It looked expensive. And it was still in the original protective wrapping.

He studied her loosely flowing hair and pink cheeks. "Where and when did you get this?"

Bridgett beamed. "At the baby boutique in town, when I first decided to foster-adopt. I knew getting a baby could happen suddenly, so I wanted to be ready."

That made sense, knowing how sentimental she was. Starting it now—when she was far from being awarded permanent custody—did not.

He put his empty dishes in the dishwasher. Turning back to her, he clamped his arms across his chest. "Why are you doing this?"

Her chin took on the stubborn tilt he was beginning to know so well. "So, no matter what happens to him, Robby will know that he was loved his very first days." She jerked in a quavering breath. "It won't just be the story of how he was found in a cardboard shipping box with only a little puppy to watch over him." Her voice caught.

It was a moment before she could go on. "Though I'm hoping he never learns that part."

Cullen's heart clutched. "Me, too."

Next to the album was an open file folder. It held the fostering paperwork along with the note that Robby had been found with. "You're planning to put that in, too?"

Bridgett stiffened in indignation. "This letter proves that his mother loved him and wanted the best for him." She studied him, scowling. "I can see you don't approve. You think that I shouldn't be doing this at all, at least, not now," she guessed in obvious disappointment.

"I think you're setting yourself up to be terribly hurt if this dream of raising Robby as your own child all goes south." Which it still could.

Bridgett glared at him resentfully. "Don't you think if Robby and Riot had any other family who wanted to keep them, that family would certainly have realized the two were missing by now and be looking for them?"

Cullen didn't know how to respond, except to say, "You would certainly hope so."

Fortunately, in the meantime, there were things he could do to protect them all.

"HEY," CULLEN SAID, to his brother Dan, later the same afternoon. "I'm glad you could take the time to meet with me."

Dan stepped out of his patrol car. "I was headed in this direction, anyway. What's up?"

Cullen took the tack off his horse and led him into the stable. "I'm worried about Bridgett."

His brother lounged in the center aisle. "Taking care of a baby and a puppy—and putting up with you—too much for her?"

Cullen made sure his horse had fresh water and then shut the stall door. "Ha, ha."

Dan accompanied him to the tack room. "You are a handful. According to Mom, all of us kids are."

Except he wasn't one of Rachel's kids, Cullen thought, putting the saddle away.

He was a stepson.

Not that Rachel treated him any differently. In fact, she treated him like he was her biological son, too.

Aware this wasn't something he could discuss with his law-enforcement half brother, Cullen sobered. "Bridgett thinks it's destiny that she was the one who found Robby and Riot."

As far as he was concerned, whimsical thinking like that only brought trouble.

Dan shrugged and walked back out into the sunshine with him. "Maybe it was."

"She's got her heart set on adopting them both and being their mom. She's even making a baby book."

Dan leaned up against the pasture fence. "You're worried someone is going to come and claim him?"

"Or maybe won't now—only to show up later when her heart is really involved. Which is why we have to solve as much of the mystery as we can, as soon as we can."

"You've got some more ideas on how to go about this?"

Cullen nodded. "Do you remember me talking about the original Riot?"

His brother squinted. "You mean, aside from that one time, the first year you were with us?"

It had been an awful, awkward, emotional conversation, with him fighting back tears. Cullen bit down his embarrassment. "Yeah."

"No. You've never mentioned him since. Or anything the least bit personal to you."

"Exactly," Cullen said, knowing it to be true. "Yet someone—who left the baby and named their puppy after mine—knows about him. They must, because that's not a common dog name. And that's gotten me to thinking. I vaguely recall telling a few stories about my Riot to a group of people at some point during the last year."

Dan straightened. "Seriously?"

"It wasn't anything I'd planned. The subject of dogs came up and someone asked me point-blank if I'd ever had one. Before I knew it, I was talking about the virtues of having a dog, as a boy, on the various cattle ranches where my mom and I lived. How he made every new place immediately seem like home."

Dan rubbed his jaw. "Wow. I think that's the most I've ever heard you talk about anything but cattle ranching."

Cullen gave the other man a deadpan look. "I was hoping you might be able to help me figure out where or when this soliloquy of mine happened."

Dan shrugged. "I don't know. Sounds like a gathering that was at least semi-social."

"Yeah." *But where? And when?*

"You think figuring this out will lead you to who left the baby?"

"It's possible. One thing is for sure," Cullen admitted worriedly, "I'm not sure Bridgett will recover if she loses Robby and Riot."

Nor was it likely she'd want to spend a lot of time hanging out with him. Or at the Western Cross, given the painful memories that would likely generate. He'd be nothing but a reminder of all she'd lost.

Dan studied him. "What about you? How are you going to feel if someone comes forward to claim them?"

Bummed. He'd gotten used to having the baby and puppy around. Bridgett, too. Bridgett *especially*. Aware his brother was still waiting for his answer, Cullen adopted a poker face. "I'll be fine."

Dan studied him in disappointment. "Robby's really not your kid?"

Cullen wondered how many times he would have to repeat this. "Really not." But he was beginning to wish they were his family. Not one to dwell on things he could not change, however, he pushed on. "Anyway, that's the second reason I called you. I wanted to find out if there were any updates on the search."

"Actually—" Dan brightened "—there are."

DAN ONLY WANTED to go over it once, so they went up to the ranch house. Bridgett was in the kitchen, typing away madly on her laptop computer. Robby was sleeping in his Moses basket nearby. The smell of still-brewing coffee and home-baked cookies filled the room. Additional baked goods lined the counter. "More gifts of food?" he asked, stepping inside.

Bridgett smiled happily, still typing. "And baby and puppy things. It's tradition, when there's a newborn or new pet in the house."

He was beginning to see that.

A constant influx of unexpected visitors was not something he usually liked. On the other hand, their generosity made going into town—for some of the very things that had been dropped off—an avoidable chore. With the virtual auction coming up, he was glad not to have to spend the extra time commuting back and forth.

Not sure what he was interrupting, Cullen asked, "Is this an okay time to talk?"

Bridgett saw his brother, in uniform, come in after him. She closed her laptop and gestured for the two men to help themselves to a late-afternoon treat. "Sure. I was just filling out more bank paperwork."

With a nod of thanks, Cullen and Dan helped themselves to cookies. "I thought that was a closed avenue."

"The local bank is," she said, taking a peanut-butter cookie for herself. "I'm trying one of those online services that promise to provide a loan to *every kind* of borrower."

Or, at least, take your application fee and squash your hopes, Cullen thought.

Bridgett continued cheerfully, "They've promised an answer within forty-eight to seventy-two hours, provided I give them all the necessary documentation. The sellers agreed to give me one more try to obtain financing, so I'm going for it."

She walked across the room to the Moses basket, tenderly checked on Robby. Seeing he was starting to wake, she checked her watch then went to get a bottle of formula from the fridge.

"What's up?" She tossed the words over her shoulder, giving Cullen a fine view of her slender waist and delectable backside. She was beautiful in a nurse's uniform, but she also looked damn fine in jeans and a form-fitting red knit shirt that clung to her midriff and buttoned up the front.

Too fine for him not to want her.

Apparently oblivious to his amorous thoughts, Dan leaned against the counter, arms folded in front of him. He looked at them both seriously. "I wanted to update you both on the progress of the investigation thus far. We dusted the shipping box the baby was found in and came up with fourteen different sets of fingerprints. None of them matched anything in the integrated fingerprint identification system."

"What kind of box was it, anyway?" Cullen asked, aware he'd never actually seen it.

Bridgett gave the name of a popular internet shipping company.

Cullen watched her set the bottle in the electric warmer that Rachel had thoughtfully brought over the previous day. "Did it have an address label?" he asked.

"Yes," Dan confirmed.

Bridgett nodded. "But both the address and tracking numbers had been marked through with permanent black ink."

Cullen felt a stab of disappointment. He wanted to get this mystery cleared up, so they could all move forward, unencumbered, a permanent home for Robby and Riot and Bridgett decided upon.

"There's no way to uncover what was beneath?" Realizing the coffee had finally finished brewing, he gave his brother a mug then poured two more. His fingers grazed the silky softness of Bridgett's as he handed hers over. Fueling memories of their passionate lovemaking the day before and furthering his desire to bring them closer yet, in ways that went far beyond this situation they found themselves in.

Dan answered Cullen's question matter-of-factly. "We sent it to the crime lab for analysis. They said they would do their best but weren't encouraging."

"What about the clinics and hospitals?" Bridgett asked, stirring some cream into her coffee, her soft pink lips taking on an even more serious curve. "Anything there?"

"Nothing yet," Dan admitted candidly, "but we're still hopeful."

Bridgett nodded, sipping her coffee as she and Dan exchanged knowing looks. Cullen felt like the odd man out. She explained. "We know by the way the entire umbilical cord was left hanging that Robby was not born with any medical personnel present. Otherwise, that would have been handled much differently. So his mother could have similar post-birth problems that would have compelled her to seek medical help."

"So, why not put out the news about what happened and publically encourage her to come in for the proper medical care she needs?"

"Because that would likely have the opposite effect and could keep her in hiding," Bridgett said firmly.

Dan drained his mug. "The department agrees. The best thing to do is stay the course. Plus, we're starting to get a few tips."

"Like...?" Cullen prodded.

"An elderly resident on Spring Street noticed a car moving slowly down her street around three thirty in the morning, a few hours before Robby was found."

"Were you able to track down the car?"

"She didn't have her glasses on, so she didn't get a color, make or model. Or even part of a license plate number."

"That's disappointing," Bridgett interjected. "But did anyone else see anything?"

Dan nodded. "A few blocks over from there, a young mother, up nursing her baby, thought she heard excited teenage voices and maybe a dog barking outside around 4:00 a.m. Because it was April Fool's Day, she wondered if they were attempting to get an early start and prank someone before school started. By the time she had finished nursing and went to the window, though, there was no one there. No evidence of any prank she could see."

"And that's it?" Cullen asked.

"So far. But we've quietly put the word out in the neighborhoods surrounding the fire station as well as all the high schools in the area. So if there is more information to be had," Dan promised, "I'm sure we'll get it shortly."

As HIS BROTHER LEFT, Cullen's phone rang. He paused before moving to answer it, ready to let the machine take it. Then he asked Bridgett, "Need any help?"

Bridgett took Robby from the Moses basket and nestled the cooing baby close. "I've got this," she said softly. "You just take care of business. Your office phone has been ringing off the hook all day."

"Thanks." Cullen strode to the front of the house.

By the time he returned, forty-five minutes later, Bridgett was putting a sleeping Robby back down.

Regret welled within him. He had hoped to be able to hold the baby a little bit, before he went back to sleep. How crazy was that? If he didn't watch it, he would be as attached to Robby as Bridgett was. Her heart wouldn't be the only one that was broken if the birth mother or her family did suddenly show up to claim him.

Finished with the baby, she grabbed the leash off the hook by the back door and clipped it to Riot's collar. Wordlessly she led the puppy outdoors. Cullen followed as Riot sniffed and circled, looking for the perfect patch of grass.

"You are such a good puppy!" she praised as Riot relieved himself, all the while gazing up at her adoringly.

"Someone has been reading about dog training."

"Competition. I want to get as good as you are with him."

And he wanted to up his game where the baby was concerned. Even if they didn't get to keep Robby. Because this experience had made him realize he did want a family someday. Actually, his wish was a little more specific than that. He wanted *this* family. Foolish or not.

Being careful not to stray out of earshot of the house, Bridgett walked Riot to another patch of grass, pausing to send Cullen a concerned glance. "Is everything okay?"

"All the phone calls? Yeah. People have been preregistering for the virtual cattle auction online. They have a lot of questions."

"I meant about what your brother Dan had to say."

"Oh." He exhaled. Funny how well she could read him after such a short period of time. "I'm just frustrated," he admitted, pursing his lips.

A mirthful sparkle appeared in her eyes.

He tilted his head. "Not that kind of frustrated," he muttered, edging closer. Although, if she kept looking at him with that same sweet innocence, he might soon be.

"Good to know," she said softly, her gaze remaining playful while her cheeks turned the same pink as when they made love.

His body reacted at the memory.

He longed to kiss her. But with them standing outside, the dog on the leash, he wouldn't be able to give the embrace the time and attention he wanted. And when he kissed her again, and he *would* kiss her, he wanted to be able to take his time about it. Give her the care she deserved.

Aware she was still waiting, he cleared his throat. "It's driving me crazy, trying to figure out how Riot Junior is connected to Riot Senior and me."

"I'm sure it will come to you eventually."

Would it? he wondered, his frustration returning. It hadn't so far.

"Maybe if you had some photos to look at, it might jog your memory." She snapped her fingers. "Oh, right. You don't know where they are. Do you?"

Chapter Eight

Bridgett had grown up with two brothers, so she recognized masculine evasion when she saw it. And she had caught Cullen Reid McCabe red-handed.

He offered a sexy half smile, making her feel more beautiful and womanly than anyone ever had. "It's not that I don't know where they are, exactly. I do. They're in a storage locker in Laramie."

Bridgett forced herself to concentrate on the mystery they were trying to solve, not what she wished would happen between her and Cullen. Again. "EZ Time Storage Lockers?"

His glance roved her slowly. He seemed to be contemplating how to bring them closer than they already were. She thrilled at the notion.

"The one and only."

Reminding herself to keep her guard up, lest they further complicate an already ridiculously complex and emotional situation, she step back a pace. "That's where I put my stuff when I had to move out of my apartment."

He took her hand in his, letting her know with a look and a touch they had nothing to be wary about. They were adult enough to handle whatever happened next, with Robby and Riot. And most especially, the two of them.

Tightening his fingers around hers, he drew her closer

still. His voice dropped to a sexy rasp. "Guess that makes us neighbors there, as well as temporary housemates."

"And friends?" she clarified, before she could stop herself.

He gave her a thoughtful once-over. His steady regard gentled. "At the very least."

She glanced up at the ruggedly handsome contours of his face, appreciating his strength and determination as well as his indomitable spirit. The way he made her feel as if she were no longer in a waiting-mode, but suddenly living every moment of her life to the fullest. Yet so much of him was still a mystery to her. She needed to know more, before she could allow herself to get any closer to him. She needed him to want to tell her. "So what's the problem in running over there—besides the fact it will take us about thirty minutes?"

He shrugged, disengaging their linked fingers, maddeningly reserved once again. "I can't just walk in and walk back out." He tucked his thumbs in the belt loops on either side of his fly. "I'm going to have to hunt through a bunch of old moving boxes to find them."

Her turn to shrug. "That's fine with me."

"It'll be a pain," he predicted.

They took Riot back inside. She went straight to the sink and washed her hands. "Won't it be worth it, though, if looking at old photos jogs your memory in some way?"

His grimace let her know that this was a trip down memory lane he did not want to take. "You have no idea how disorganized and dusty it is in there."

She propped her hands on her hips. With a tilt of her head, she surveyed him up and down. "Are you a secret packrat?" she teased, in an attempt to lessen his reluctance.

He stroked his chin with his thumb and index fingers.

"Could be," he drawled, sizing her up right back. "You never know about us Texas cowboys."

"But you will go, right?"

He exhaled. "Right."

Aware she had almost finished her online mortgage application and had until midnight to send it in, Bridgett bypassed her computer and went to get her bag and phone. When those were ready to go, she started packing a diaper bag.

Still mulling over his reluctance, she remarked, "From the look of things here, I thought you were one of those super organized, everything in its place kind of guys."

Another shrug. "Kind of had to be."

"Because those were the rules, growing up?"

The distant look in his eyes faded. "No. My mom was laid-back in that respect." He smiled, remembering, "She always let me keep my room as messy and full of mementos as I wanted it to be. It was foster care that changed me. Taught me to leave as small a footprint as possible, if I wanted to stay under the radar. And I did."

She thought about how miserable that must have been for him. Working to keep the pity out of her voice, she said, "And when you moved to Laramie?"

His eyes shuttered. "It seemed like a good idea to keep that habit."

"Just in case…?"

His lips thinned. "Frank and Rachel decided I was more trouble than I was worth."

"Oh, Cullen," she said softly.

He moved away before she could comfort him. "But as you can see," he said over his shoulder, striding into his office to turn off his own computers, "everything worked out."

Had it?

It seemed like there was still a barrier between Cullen and the rest of his McCabe family, just as there was between him and her.

The walls guarding his heart were starting to come down, at least between the two of them. But they had a long way to go if they were ever going to be more than temporary housemates and one-time lovers.

"Well, I must say you have amazing organizational talents," Bridgett continued lightly in an attempt to get the conversation back on safer ground.

He moved away from his desk and spread his hands wide. "I can't take all the credit for how good this place looks. My half sister, Lulu, helped me move in. She's very particular in how she likes things decorated and arranged. All I do to keep it looking this way is put everything back in its preassigned place."

"Do you have a housekeeper?" She hadn't seen one thus far.

He shook his head.

She studied him in surprise. "You keep this place this tidy all on your own?"

"Yes, I do."

Wow. "You are way too humble, cowboy."

One brow went up.

Laying a hand across her chest in true Texas-belle fashion, Bridgett drawled, "You are a woman's dream man."

He chuckled, as she'd meant him to. "Because I can cook and clean?"

She shook her head and let out a low laugh. "And so many other things."

"You'll have to show me just how dreamy I am, sometime." He leaned in to kiss her, sweetly, tenderly.

On impulse, she kissed him back. His kiss was every bit as magical as it had been before, and her body jolted from the sheer bliss of it. She heard herself make a sound of pure pleasure and opened her mouth to the pressure of his, aware she hadn't made out like this, like kissing was an end in and of itself, since she didn't know when.

Satisfaction emanated from him, too. With the flat of his hand against her spine, he pressed her closer, until her skin sizzled and her nipples budded against the hardness of his chest.

Her knees went weak.

And still he kissed her, until she was tingling all over and so dizzy she could barely stand, until desire unfurled like a ribbon inside her and her thighs were trembling.

And she knew, unless they stopped—now—they'd never make it to the storage locker.

Reluctantly, she pressed a hand to the center of his chest. He drew back, content, yet wanting more. And, as she looked up at him, she wondered how he could not be aware just how gorgeous a guy he was. With his chiseled features, thick, curly dark hair, navy blue eyes and tall muscled body, he was masculine perfection come to life. Physically, anyway. Emotionally they still had some barriers to take down, and connections to build. But they were working on it. For the moment, that was enough.

BRIDGETT AND CULLEN dropped off the baby with her sister-in-law, Violet, and made plans to join her and her brother Gavin later for dinner. That accomplished, they proceeded to EZ Time Storage Lockers.

"You weren't kidding. This is a bit of a mess," Bridgett remarked in surprise as they walked into the nine by twelve foot temperature-controlled room. The lights overhead came on automatically when the door was opened. Wanting privacy, Bridgett shut the door to the interior corridor behind them.

"Yeah, I've never gotten around to organizing things."

Because it was too painful?

Bridgett could understand that.

Cullen walked past a flowered sofa and wing chair. Past a dining table and four chairs. Twin and double beds, two bureaus, a nightstand and a coffee table.

It was, Bridgett thought, a sad summary of a life.

He approached the stack of thirty or so boxes. Exhaled roughly. "Plus, it wasn't a stellar packing job, by any means. I was lucky the social worker assigned to me after my mom died made sure everything we had, in the home we were living in, was put in storage for me until I came of age and could decide what I wanted to do with it."

"Have you been through it at all?"

He shook his head, his expression conveying how much he had been dreading it.

Squaring his broad shoulders, Cullen demonstrated he was up to the task. "No time like the present."

Twenty minutes later, they had opened up all of the cartons. A lot of them held linens and women's clothing. There were a few boyish toys that Robby might one day enjoy, as well as a very out-of-date video game system. "This might be worth something if it still works."

A corner of his mouth crooked up. "Maybe as a museum piece."

And, finally, they found a cloth-covered box of photos. She handed it to him.

He made his way back to the sofa and sat down. Motioned for her to join him. She dragged the coffee table over so they could sit with their feet up. "You sure you don't want to do this alone?" She knew how an image, long unseen, could catch you like an arrow through the heart. "'Cause my storage unit is just one row over, and I could also use a few things."

He patted the place right next to him. "Sit. I know you're curious. This way I won't have to do it twice."

She plopped down next to him, then abruptly stopped, staring at the butchered pictures. "What happened to these?" she asked, aghast.

He sighed at the oddly cropped photos. "My mom did it. She was all about the Boyfriend of the Moment. When he eventually failed to become her Prince Charming, and they all did, she couldn't bear any reminders, so she cut them out of the photos."

Noting that, even as a kid, Cullen had been tall and good-looking, already growing into the ruggedly masculine man he would become, Bridgett quipped, "Apparently that was in the days *before* photoshopping became popular?"

He grinned, sharing in the black humor. "Actually, I think my mom rather enjoyed erasing them that way."

Bridgett could imagine it had all been very dramatic. And undoubtedly quite upsetting for Cullen, when he was a kid. She reached over and took his hand, offering wordless comfort. "How did you feel about it?"

The reserve back in his expression, he set a stack of butchered childhood photos aside. "I wish she'd had some pictures taken of just the two of us, so we could have kept those and tossed out the rest."

"It definitely would have been a lot simpler," Bridgett agreed gently.

And less melodramatic.

He exhaled, accepting the past for what it was. "But that wasn't the way she worked, so…" He sat back, propping his feet on the coffee table in front of them.

She got comfortable, putting her feet up, too. "Did you like the men she dated?" Because if he hadn't, that would have really been awful.

He stretched his arm along the back of the sofa and protectively curved a strong arm about her shoulders. He lowered his voice to a husky murmur that did nothing to lessen the impact of his warm, sexy touch.

"Most of them were really nice. Kind. All of them cowboys on the various ranches where she worked as a chef. They all took me under their wing, even the gruff ones." He looked down at her as, feeling a wave of compassion for him, she nestled in the curve of his body. "I think they felt sorry for me, not having a dad, having a mom who was more interested in her love life than her child."

That had to have stung.

He reached out and smoothed a strand of her hair. "So whenever we inevitably left the ranch where we'd been living, it was usually harder for me to say goodbye to everyone than it was for my mom."

No wonder he worked so hard to keep from forging ties that might hurt if they one day had to be broken. With a sigh, she snuggled in even closer. "I'm sorry."

He nodded, the muscles of his powerful chest straining against the soft blue chambray of his shirt.

"So where did Riot Senior come in?" she asked, as their eyes met, and everything around them began to fade.

He smiled affectionately, recalling. "I was six the night he showed up on our doorstep in the snow, on Christmas Eve, begging to be let in."

She could imagine the joy he'd felt. It was probably one of the highlights of his youth. She swallowed around the growing knot of emotion in her throat. "Did your mom put him there?" she asked, knowing she wasn't the only one who needed kissing and holding and loving.

"She said it was Santa. I think it was Buck, her boyfriend at the time. He was always saying every boy should have a dog."

She met his wry smile. "But your mom let you keep him."

"I don't think she had a lot of choice." He removed his arm from her shoulders and thumbed through the few photos of him and his dog, a big, long-haired black, brown and white mutt. "I was completely in love with the little fella. Buck taught me how to care for him and train him."

"He sounds like a great guy."

Cullen nodded fondly, "He would have made a great dad for me. But Mom got tired of him. Said he wasn't romantic enough and moved us on. Again. But this time, I got to take Riot Senior with me, so it wasn't so bad."

"Did you ever stay in touch with Buck?"

His gaze narrowed and Bridgett felt her heart break for him all over again. "No. Buck and Mom both thought it would be better if we all made a clean break, so we did."

Bridgett ached to ease his pain.

"You don't think that Buck could be responsible for the new puppy in some way?"

"Actually, the thought crossed my mind. So I did some checking on my own and found out he died of a heart attack five years ago at the same ranch where he had always worked."

Bridgett shared his sadness. For a moment, they fell silent. Finally, she asked, "And there's no one else? No other ex-boyfriend of your mom's who would have given you a puppy and a baby?"

"No. No one."

She reached over and covered his hand with her own, both their hands resting on his muscular thigh. "It's too bad you didn't know about Frank sooner," Bridgett observed eventually. She turned to look him in the eye. "It seems like that would have made your childhood so much better."

"But I didn't," he confided quietly. "And we can't go back, Bridgett, and redo the past, much as we might want to. We can only go forward."

And, given the intent way he was suddenly looking at her, she realized on a quick inhalation of breath, going forward meant one thing.

She had hoped to wait until her situation was more settled before they did this again.

However, the way he had opened up his heart to her, the way he looked at her now, so full of yearning, changed all that. He was inviting her in, and the truth was, she wanted in. Already all of her senses were in overdrive and he hadn't even kissed her yet.

He leaned in and her lips parted. He pressed a light kiss to one corner of her mouth, and then another to the other side. Trembling with pleasure, she wreathed her arms about his neck. Their breaths mingled. And then his mouth was moving over hers, creating frissions of delight. His hands were beneath her blouse, cupping the weight of her breasts, teasing the taut nipples with his thumbs. And still they kissed, tongues and lips tangling, the caresses hot and hard, slow and soft, again and again and again, until making out felt like the most intimate thing they could ever do.

Heavens, the man knew how to kiss! How to make her want him. Not just like this, but in every other way, too…

"Not here," he whispered finally, lifting his head.

She was too far gone to stop. Too far gone to *want* to stop. "Yes, here," she insisted, just as fiercely, shifting so they were both prone on the sofa.

Giving in to the passion flooding them both, he tugged off her jeans and panties. She divested him of his. And then his hands and mouth began a downward journey. She fisted her hands in his hair, afraid he would stop. He didn't. Not until she was shuddering with sensation and crying out his name. And then he was moving again, swiftly now, finding the condom, rolling it on.

Feelings sweeping through her, she wrapped her arms and legs around him, urging him home. And when he entered her, thrusting into her, long and slow, taking her to a whole new level of need, he made her feel so utterly… taken. And that was what she wanted, too. So much.

She was his. He was hers.

And still they kissed as he brought them closer and closer, making her moan and cry out, until she lost track of where he ended and she began. All she knew was that everything around her was lost in the hot, intensely erotic pull of the two of them, the inevitable ascent to ecstasy and the slower, softer, oh so satisfying fall back.

AS THE AFTERSHOCKS FADED, Cullen went still, waiting to see what Bridgett would do. She didn't pull away from him, the way she had the first time they'd made love. She didn't snuggle closer, either. He wasn't surprised about that. She was an elusive woman.

Still holding her in his arms, he pressed a kiss to her temple. "So," he prodded finally, knowing their situation was complicated. But complicated was okay when it led to results like this. He just had to convince her of that. He shifted so he could see her face. "Was that a pity move, on your part?"

She lifted her head so he could gaze into her pretty green eyes. "You mean did I make love to you because I felt sorry for you?" Her voice was filled with surprise.

Not sure it mattered to him if she had—since it had brought them closer—he sifted his hand reassuringly through the silky mane of her hair. "Did you?" he asked curiously.

She shifted against him, and he felt himself grow hard again. Rolling onto her side, she spread her hands across his chest. "I definitely felt for you and what you'd been through."

He knew that. He had noticed her compassion.

"I also felt closer to you, because you trust me enough to confide in me that way."

He grinned. "So, is this the part where you tell me that now I've seen your pictures, you will show me yours?"

She regarded him with wide-eyed interest, both surprised and pleased. "You want to see my family albums? What ones I have, anyway?"

"Only fair." He wanted to know what she had been like as a child, before he moved to Laramie, Texas. That was unusual, too. Generally, he liked to stay in the here and now. Not think about the past. Or the future. But with her, he wanted to know everything.

Smiling, Bridgett extricated herself. She reached for her clothes and shimmied into her bra and panties. "They're in the storage locker with my stuff."

He lay back, watching, while she put on her blouse and her jeans. Damn, she was beautiful. Kind. Smart, and every kind of wonderful, too.

"I know right where they are, so I can slip over to my rental unit and get them. We won't have time to go through them right now, though. We're already close to being late for dinner with Violet and Gavin."

Reluctantly, he rose and began to dress. Doing what a guy always did when he was interested in a woman. Try to nail down their next time together, before the current interlude ended. "Later, then?" he made her promise.

Bridgett grinned, nodding. "It's a date."

Chapter Nine

It's a date. Why had she said that? Bridgett chastised herself silently. She and Cullen were not dating. Sleeping together, yes, but dating? If she didn't want him to think she was one of those women who would hook up with a guy once or twice and then be ready to move in with him permanently, she would have to be more careful.

He sent her a sideways glance. "Stop beating yourself up."

"For what?"

"Showing me your feelings."

Bridgett ducked her head and rummaged around for her boots. "I didn't."

"Yes, you did," he said, giving her a frankly admiring glance. "And unless you want your brother and sister-in-law to see 'em, too, you better apply a little more lip gloss and run a brush through your hair."

Bridgett rushed to her shoulder bag, to find a mirror. "I really look that ravished?"

He shrugged. "To me you do."

Bridgett opened a small compact of blusher and groaned. She did look all…tousled. In fact, her skin seemed to be glowing from the inside out. Same as the rest of her. "I knew you were trouble the moment I met you," she grumbled teasingly.

He extracted a comb from his wallet and tidied up, too. "Right back at you, kid."

Short minutes later, they were on their way.

Gavin had just arrived home. As soon as greetings were given, Bridgett rushed over to see Robby, who was in his cozy little infant carrier, sleeping peacefully. "How has he been?"

Violet smiled. "He was a little dreamboat."

"He is a very cute kid," Gavin agreed, as they all sat down to dinner. "I can see why you're so attached to him, Bridgett."

Bridgett helped herself to some salad. "But you're worried."

"He's not actually up for adoption. Is he?" Gavin paused and looked at Cullen. "Is he even going to be?"

Cullen held her brother's level, assessing gaze with one of his own. "If you're asking…he is not my baby."

Biologically, anyway, Bridgett thought. It seemed emotionally the two had already bonded.

"And yet you've stepped in," Gavin said, his voice hard.

Cullen passed the breadbasket. "It's the right thing to do. In fact—" he met her brother's gaze equably "—I would help care for Robby and Riot even if they hadn't been left with a note, charging me with the responsibility."

Bridgett knew Cullen well enough now to realize how true that was. He might act all tough and gruff on the outside sometimes, especially around those who might be seeking to take advantage, but inside he was kind and big hearted. Tender and loving to a fault. The perfect father for Robby and Riot.

The perfect husband for her?

Now who was jumping the gun? she thought, hanging her head. For a moment, everyone ate their salad in awkward silence.

Finally, Violet looked at Cullen, one McCabe to another, interjecting kindly. "We went through something similar with our first child, Ava."

Glad to have the focus off her and Cullen, Bridgett explained what had happened while Cullen was living out of state. "Gavin and Violet were named legal guardians of a premature infant whose mother died in childbirth. They hardly knew each other at the time."

Violet took Gavin's hand. The love between them was palpable. "It was while taking care of little Ava, seeing her through her medical crisis, that we fell in love."

Gavin squeezed his doctor wife's hand affectionately, then started on his lasagna. "Circumstances were a little different, though. Since from the very beginning you and I knew we could adopt Ava, if we chose."

"If we passed social service's home study," Violet amended.

Happily, that wasn't a problem here. "I've already passed mine," Bridgett said. "Two years ago, when I was approved to foster-adopt."

Violet looked at Cullen. "Is that something you're interested in doing?" she asked.

Cullen continued devouring his pasta. "Never gave it any thought until now."

Bridgett was sure that was true.

"What about marriage?" Gavin asked. "Are you interested in that?"

Bridgett winced. This was nothing new. She knew Gavin felt it was his duty as the male head of the family to protect all three of his sisters. But there was no way she was letting Gavin chase Cullen away, the way he had every man he thought might potentially hurt her. There was simply too much at stake. He needed to back off.

The two men continued staring each other down. "I

might be inclined to get hitched, if the right woman came along," Cullen shot back evenly.

Gavin stared back at him, waiting it seemed for a declaration that never came.

Which meant what? Bridgett wondered.

Cullen wasn't really serious about her? Or he was, but—like most strong, silent men— didn't feel the need to explain himself?

There was no clue from the impassive look on his handsome face.

Nothing that Gavin could jump on, either.

The rest of the meal was eaten in tense silence, and stilted small talk. Unable to stand the disquiet any longer, Bridgett thanked them both for a lovely meal, as did Cullen, and begged off, right after dessert.

"I AM SO SORRY," Bridgett moaned as they drove away, short minutes later.

"Why?" Cullen asked, his muscular frame filling the interior of the pickup truck. That time of night, there wasn't a lot of traffic, and he went through one green light, then another. "They love you. They want what is best for you. They just don't think it is me."

Bridgett straightened. "Pull over."

His brow furrowed. "What?"

Bridgett pointed to an empty parking lot, next to an office building on the outskirts of town. "Pull over! I want you to look me in the eye when I say this." She waited until he had complied before she continued. "My family doesn't know what is best for me, Cullen. I get to decide that."

He met her gaze wryly, his eyes dark and heated. "Really? And what have you decided?"

"That we do not have to decide anything right now,"

she said firmly. She waved a hand. "Beyond, of course, figuring out how I am going to get my living conditions straightened out before the foster placement decision on Robby and Riot."

His big body relaxed. He reached over to take her hand. "What can I do to help?"

"Take care of Robby and Riot while I finish my online mortgage application this evening?"

"I'm on it," he assured her. "No problem."

And it wasn't.

Until just before midnight, seconds after her application had been emailed in. He was sitting on the sofa, his cheek pressed against the top of Robby's head, Riot curled up at his feet. He had the pictures of his first dog spread across his lap.

She eased down next to them. Then turned so she could sit kitty-corner to him. "Any luck remembering?"

Frustration curved the corners of his lips. "No. I talk to so many groups of people. Potential buyers who come for a tour of the ranch. Cattlemen's meetings around the state…"

"And don't forget the career fair at the high school," Bridgett interjected helpfully. "You and I were both present for that."

Cullen's brow furrowed. "Actually, I didn't just visit Laramie County High School. I spoke at two in San Angelo last fall, as well. In fact, I've done them wherever I lived."

A mixture of hope and dread sparked inside Bridgett. "You think that might have been where you discussed Riot?"

"Maybe. I mean the conversations with business people tend to stay on track. With high school kids, looking to choose their life's work, the conversations can go all over the place. And I do mean all over the place!"

Bridgett grinned ruefully. "I know what you mean. I was once asked if the best way to marry a handsome doctor was to become a nurse or a physician. Which one did I think would give a girl a better chance?"

Cullen winced. "What'd you say?"

"That I wouldn't know because I wanted to marry for love, not profession."

Approval shone in his eyes. "Good call."

"What about you?" Bridgett asked curiously, loving the intimacy that sprung up between them. "What was your weirdest question?"

"Boxers or briefs. Definitely the most uncomfortable."

"What did you say?"

He made a comical face. "Next question!"

Bridgett laughed softly. "Can't say I blame you."

Robby sighed in his sleep. Cullen snuggled the infant closer and bussed the top of his little head.

They looked so sweet together, so right, it nearly broke Bridgett's heart.

Oblivious to the tenderness welling up inside her, Cullen continued, "It's par for the course—a lot of teenage girls show up to hear the cowboys speak. But they also want to know things like if it's lonely on a ranch. Do we have to work all the time, or do we still have time for fun? Is it a good place to raise kids? Things like that."

"So, maybe...that is where you talked about Riot."

He nodded in agreement, still mulling over the possibilities. "But at which high school? And when?"

Bridgett had no idea.

She did know, however, that her life had just gotten more precarious than ever.

CULLEN CALLED DAN first thing the next morning to let him know what he and Bridgett were thinking.

"Well?" Bridgett asked anxiously when he hung up the phone. She stepped away from the breakfast she was cooking.

"Dan said he doesn't think it was Laramie High, because he's already talked to the principal and guidance counselors there, and they haven't had any girls get pregnant. But he'll call the two other high schools in San Angelo, where I spoke. See what he can find out."

She sauntered nearer, hands in her pockets. She had dried her hair after her shower that morning, leaving it long and loose and straight. But he liked it tousled and wavy, too. "How long does he think that will take?" she asked quietly.

He wrapped his arm about her shoulders, and she turned toward him, the warm abundance of her breasts brushing his chest. He pushed away the urge to explore her soft, womanly curves. "A couple of days, minimum. Everyone in the area is out for the week, on spring break, which includes the administrators."

She bit her lip, sighed and rested her head against his shoulder. "So it will be next week before we hear anything."

He pressed a kiss into her hair. "Most likely."

"I guess that's good news and bad news. Good, in that it gives us more time with Robby and Riot. Bad—" her eyes suddenly shimmered with unexpected tears "—in that if this lead does take us to Robby's birth mother, it could also mean the situation is about to get a lot more complicated." After giving the scrambled eggs another stir, she set down the spatula, looking all the more anxious. "Making my chances of foster-adopting Robby and Riot a lot more improbable."

He paused, surprised she had voiced a negative thought out loud. Up to now, she had been resolute in her view that this would all work out in her favor. Guilt came at him, swift and hard. It was because of him, somehow, that she was going through this. If it didn't work out, he would likely be to blame.

Watching her wipe her lashes with the pads of her index fingers, he stepped closer. "Are you going to be able to do this? Give the baby and puppy up if it comes to that?"

Embarrassed by the show of emotion, she turned away. "Are you?"

He caught her by the shoulders and spun her back to face him. "I'm serious, Bridgett."

"So am I." She stalked to the oven and removed a pan of fluffy, golden-brown biscuits. Then she piled freshly prepared sausage patties onto a serving platter. He helped her by doing the same with the scrambled eggs.

She set the dishes on the island, then went back to the cupboard to get out plates and utensils. "Do you honestly think that Robby would be better off with someone who would leave him in a cardboard box, with only a well-intentioned puppy to guard him, instead of with me?"

Her lower lip trembled.

She sloshed juice over the sides of the glasses, then set the pitcher down in frustration, looking at him. "I want you to be able to clear your name, Cullen. I know how important that is to you. But after that," she said fiercely, unable to contain her emotions any longer, "I want what's best for Robby and for Riot. And that means keeping them *with us*." She started, as astonished as he was at what she had let slip out. "Well, of course, I mean me."

She circled the island and slipped onto a stool.

"You know what I'm trying to say here," Bridgett amended hastily.

Yes, Cullen thought, *I do, because I have been thinking and wishing and hoping for the very same thing. Even though I know it's not likely to happen.*

Sighing, he sat down to eat, too. "I think you're right to be concerned. You could be in for a fight, when it comes to custody of the baby and the puppy, particularly if Robby has blood relatives who don't know about him yet and do want to raise him."

"Should kin with blood ties always win out?"

Cullen fed her a forkful of egg. "Not necessarily, not in my view. But to the court, it could be the deciding factor."

She huffed in frustration. "But don't you think that if help from the birth mother's family were readily available that Robby's birth mother would have already gone to them, given the baby and puppy over, instead of acting in such a desperate manner?"

"It had to be very hard for the birth mother, leaving Robby and Riot the way she did, even if she thought I would follow through on the written request, claim them and keep them safe and happy."

They were silent, brooding.

Bridgett broke a biscuit in half. "Or maybe the birth mother just wasn't thinking straight and underestimated her family. And they do want Robby." Her voice broke. "And Cullen, if that's the case…"

He slanted her a brief, consoling look. "Then the court will decide what is best for him, and you'll deal with whatever their decision is. Because in the end, Bridgett, you only want one thing. Same as me."

"What is best for Robby and Riot," she surmised on a heartfelt sigh.

He nodded as a contemplative silence fell.

He reached over and squeezed her hand, doing his best to comfort her. "In the meantime, you can still do everything possible to bolster your argument that a change in DCFS policy, regarding placement of newborns, is warranted. At least in your case."

She looked deep into his eyes, hanging on to his every word.

"For starters, this isn't a whim on your part. You've gone through the entire vetting process and been waiting to foster-adopt for some time now."

Bridgett brightened. "So I should use that?"

He luxuriated in the silky feel of her palm. "As well as the fact that your work as an N-ICU nurse gives you an expertise on caring for infants that few have."

Bridgett bit her lip. "That's true, but…" Her shoulders slumped. "There's still the fact I'm not married or even engaged to be."

"Maybe you don't need to be," he told her gruffly, although he was already privately wishing that would change. "You have a large and loving extended family who stand ready to help you with whatever you need."

She stood. "That's true."

Using his leverage on her hand, he drew her closer still and wrapped his arms around her. She was gorgeous and courageous and vulnerable, and he wanted to help her achieve her heart's desire more than he had ever imagined he could.

He gazed down at her tenderly. "If you present a detailed plan for caring for Robby, demonstrate to DCFS and the court how much he will benefit with you as his mommy, and reassure them that he'll never lack a loving support network of family and friends, like me, who stand ready to assist you-all…. Well, there's no way they'll be able to deny you."

Who knew he was such a cheerleader?

Bridgett splayed her hands across his chest. "You'll really be there for us?" she marveled softly. "Not just temporarily?" Her voice caught unexpectedly. "But long term?"

He brought her in for a close, comforting hug. "To support you?" he rasped, feeling abruptly emotional, too. *And help and care for you?* He savored her feminine strength. "You bet."

It wasn't what Cullen wanted, of course. To be stuck, standing on the sidelines, cheering Bridgett on. He wanted to find a way move the foster-adopt process along, get approved and get his name on the petition for custody, too.

Only the knowledge that he would be slowing down the entire process and hindering her chances to get anything resolved quickly, if he acted on his reckless desire, kept him from doing it.

Figuring, however, that he could support her behind the scenes, he called the local San Angelo newspapers. Asked if they had any photos from the high school career fairs the previous fall that hadn't been printed in the paper.

Turned out they did.

He could view them, but he'd have to go there in person. He got in the truck and headed for San Angelo.

Chapter Ten

The next few days passed swiftly. Cullen was busy prepping for the Western Cross cattle auction; Bridgett was busy marshalling her family. All four of her siblings had provided letters of recommendation, as well as detailed lists of things they could do to help her—like babysitting and grocery shopping, even laundry.

Yet she and Cullen found time to be together every night. Eating dinner. Walking Riot. Getting Robby ready for bed and giving him his last snuggle of the evening. They didn't always do all of it as one unit. And they hadn't made love since her brother Gavin had given Cullen the third degree about what his intentions toward her might be. And successfully infused Cullen with guilt.

But he still looked at her like he wanted her and treated her with gallant kindness and concern. And they always did enough to make them feel like family. And that, Bridgett knew, was dangerous. Given all that could still go wrong.

But she tried not to think about all the what-ifs, lest she start to go crazy with worry. It was enough to appreciate what they had with each other in the here and now...

"So, what do you think little fella?" Bridgett cooed to the infant in her arms, aware she had never in her life felt this content. "Do you think we should stay up a little longer and watch the sun rise or head on back upstairs and try to catch a little more shut-eye?"

Robby looked up at her adoringly. He opened his mouth, releasing a milk bubble that hovered between his rosebud lips, then yawned.

Bridgett figured, what the heck, why not stay on the back porch a few more minutes? It would give her a chance to see Cullen before he headed out, to start the ranch work with the rest of the hired hands. With the sale only four days away, there was a lot of last-minute stuff to be done.

Behind her, she heard the sound of a door opening and closing. Cullen strode out, Riot beside him.

She was still in her pajamas and robe, he was already in jeans and a work shirt and boots. He hadn't yet shaved and the stubble gave him a rugged, sexy look. "There you are," he said. "I woke up and your room was empty."

Memories of the way he had kissed her the last time they had made love sent a burning flame throughout her entire body.

Bridgett forced herself to quell the flames. He had listened to her brother's common-sense warning and taken a step back. She knew she should be sensible and do the same.

She leaned down to pet Riot, who wagged his tail gleefully. "We were trying to be quiet."

Something hot and sensual shimmered in his eyes. "How long have you been up?"

Wondering how he could look so good early in the day, Bridgett wrinkled her nose. "Since four."

Cullen took care of the dog's needs then ambled over and took a place beside Bridgett and Robby on the porch swing. "He wouldn't go back to sleep?"

Bridgett could have shifted over to give him a little more room but, liking the way her body bumped up against his, decided to remain in the strong, reassuring curve of his big frame. "He was a little restless. I think he had a little more air in his tummy than usual. It wasn't colic exactly, but…"

"Is that serious in a baby?"

Bridgett knew colic could be deadly for horses and cattle.

As she turned her head to gaze up at him, her cheek brushed his chin. "It can be sometimes. This wasn't. He just needed to be soothed and held upright."

Cullen looked like he wanted to kiss her again. She knew, because she wanted to kiss him, too.

"Good thing you're a nurse." His voice was low, gravelly.

She savored the emotion welling in her heart. Waggling her brows, she quipped, "And an increasingly skillful mom."

"That you are, darlin'." He grinned, more than willing to give credit where it was due.

Another moment of quiet contentment and suppressed sexual need passed between them.

Bridgett cleared her throat. Aware that Robby wasn't the only one who needed to be cared for. "Speaking of not sleeping," she prodded softly, "you were up awfully late last night." He'd disappeared right after dinner to check on a few things and still been hard at work in the office downstairs when she turned off her lamp at midnight.

"Yeah."

To her frustration, although they had shared a lot over the past week, nothing else was forthcoming.

"Everything proceeding okay with the presale?" she asked, wanting to help if she could. After all, he'd done so much for her.

He hesitated a moment too long. "Pretty much."

"I'd like to hear about it."

When, again, he said nothing else, she handed Robby to him. "Here. Snuggling with him will make you feel better."

He grinned, cradling the infant against his chest like a pro. "Always does." He bussed the top of Robby's head.

"So what gives?" Bridgett watched Riot—who also bore a look of concern for Cullen—curled up on the dog blanket opposite them. His silky head on his paws, he continued watching them all. Robby looked up at Cullen, too.

With such an intent audience, he finally confided with a sigh, "Over the course of the past couple of days, five potential customers have pulled out of the virtual auction."

"Is that usual?"

"No. Once someone has taken the trouble to get all the information, register as a buyer for the sale and provide a bank guarantee that funds are immediately available, they rarely withdraw."

"Did they say why?"

Another grimace. "No."

"Do you think it has to do with all the rumors?"

"Not sure what else it could be."

"People have to know you would never turn your back on a biological child!" He was far too honorable a man for that! Look how he had stepped up thus far.

"A McCabe wouldn't." He turned to give her a hard look. "A Reid might."

Angry heat welled in her chest and she stiffened. "You were *not* responsible for what your mother did to you and Frank."

"I know that." Cullen exhaled wearily. "You know that." He shook his head. "But some people think blood ties tell character, and face it…" Still cuddling Robby tenderly, he said, "…one half of mine is suspect."

Another silence fell.

Finally, Bridgett said, "I'm sorry."

"It's okay."

Except it wasn't. Not at all.

"How much of an impact will this have?" she asked gently.

"I should still be able to sell all my stock," he answered. "Purebred Hotlander cattle are in high demand."

"Why is that?"

"A number of reasons." Seeing that Robby had fallen asleep, he moved to put the baby down in the Moses basket then returned to her side. "They breed extremely well, even during a drought. The longevity of the females is very good, their udder quality outstanding, their calves are very uniform and they crossbreed well.

"Plus, the cattle producers I sell my cows and bulls to can either crossbreed their own Brangus, Braford, Beefmaster and Santa Gertrudis to mine. Or work to achieve an entire herd of purebred Hotlander cattle of their own, as I have."

Aware how cozy and domestic this all felt, cuddling next to him on the porch swing, she smiled. "So it's a win-win."

He nodded, his eyes warming as he talked about a subject he loved. "As well as a substantial investment, given the cost of Hotlander bulls and cows."

Bridgett frowned, steering them back to the problem. "Do you think all the unsubstantiated gossip will affect your bottom line?"

"Not in the end," he answered, leaning over to kiss her temple, "because if I don't get the price I want, I'll hold on and try again later."

Bridgett snuggled against him. "Wouldn't that cause a lot of talk, too?"

Another nod. "But it would be a mistake to allow the part of the herd I'm selling to go for a lower-than-usual price and have that affect future demand and profit, so…" He shrugged his broad shoulders again. "We'll see what develops."

In more than one way, Bridgett thought, as silence fell.

Knowing what she was hoping for—an ending that had all four of them as a family—she reached over and took his hand. "Well, if it helps, you weren't the only one who got bad news last night." His eyes met hers and she drew a deep breath, aware she needed him in this moment, as much as he needed her. "The online mortgage company let me know that they are turning down my request for a mortgage, too."

He did not look surprised. "I'm sorry, sweetheart."

"Yeah, me, too." She released a pensive sigh. "They said to try back in six months, once I go back to work and things are settled, and I would likely have no issue getting approved for a mortgage."

"But the house you wanted…" He shared her disappointment.

"Will be put back on the market as soon as our two Realtors read their email. I notified them last night, before I went to bed."

His gaze narrowed protectively. "You know, my offer to help you out financially still stands."

When he was potentially about to have financial woes of his own? When she had her own family standing by, ready to help her in that regard, if only she could bring herself to let them?

No, life was getting far too complicated as it was. There were decisions to be made, but not today. Not about that.

Pushing aside the mixture of gratitude and attraction mingling deep inside her, Bridgett asked cheerfully, "How about I continue to just take you up on your offer of a place to stay, for now?"

He clasped her shoulders warmly, said with the gruff affection she was beginning to know so well, "You and Robby and Riot are welcome here as long as you want, you know that."

The next thing she knew he had shifted her onto his lap. She wreathed her arms about his neck and shoulders, opened her mouth to the plundering pressure of his.

She'd never been one to focus on the here and now. To let a rush of emotion overwhelm her. Yet as sensation swept through her like a tsunami, followed by a tidal wave of yearning, she felt herself surrender to everything he wanted and needed.

And still he kissed her, as if he were in love with her, and would be for all time. As if he too felt that coming together like this was something special, that they were destined to be together like this. As a couple and as a family. And for now, she thought, as they continued to kiss and hold each other wonderingly, it was enough. It had to be.

"I COME BEARING FOOD! Is now a good time?"

Bridgett grinned at Rachel McCabe. Cullen's stepmother was wearing skinny jeans and a long sunflower-yellow tunic. She also had a pencil stuck in her upswept hair—all signs it had been a work-at-home-day for the renowned local tax attorney.

Bridgett ushered her in. "Now is a great time, especially given how much Cullen and I both love your cooking."

The older woman smiled. "He said that?"

Bridgett relieved Rachel of her burden. "He doesn't

have to. I can tell by the way he inhales whatever you bring." She inclined her head at the covered dishes on the tray. "What's on the menu tonight?"

Rachel followed her through the house. "Old-fashioned pot roast, mashed potatoes and string beans."

Glad for some female company, Bridgett grinned. "My mouth is already watering."

Rachel walked into the kitchen. She eyed the platters of cookies, muffins and various home-baked breads and fruit baskets. "Seems like I'm not the only one feeding my son these days."

Bridgett slid Rachel's gifts into the fridge. "You know how it is with new babies. Everyone wants to bring the family food." She shrugged. "Not that we're a family, but…"

"I know what you mean."

An awkward silence fell. Sensing Rachel wanted to chat, Bridgett asked, "Would you like to stay for a glass of iced tea?"

"Do you have time? I don't want to intrude."

"I'd appreciate the adult company." They peeked in on Robby and Riot, who were both sleeping, then took a seat at the kitchen island.

"I'm guessing Cullen is out on the ranch."

Having his stepmother here reminded Bridgett how much she missed her own mother. She poured tea for both of them, then set out sugar, some sliced lemon and a plate of oatmeal cookies. "He and the hired hands are sorting the cattle being put up for auction, moving them to different pastures."

Rachel nodded. "How are you doing?"

Bridgett warmed at the maternal concern. "Good. Between the baby and the puppy…" *and my thing for Cullen* "…I don't seem to have enough hours in the day, though."

"You'll get used to it."

Bridgett got up to retrieve a bunch of red grapes. "How did you manage with such a big family?"

Rachel helped herself to some fruit. "Everyone pitched in, doing chores. Lending a hand. Which was the only way I could have managed to work while they were growing up."

"You've always been a tax lawyer?"

Rachel smiled. "I have. In fact, that's how Frank and I met. Starting out, he tried to do it all, but didn't quite have a handle on how he should set up the ranch business at the Bar M. An LLC, S Corp. or straight corporation. At some point he tried all three—badly. Made a real mess of things, as far as the revenue agents were concerned. Hired me to straighten it all out. Sparks flew—because he was a McCabe and McCabes are brought up to make their own way—and he did not want to listen to me."

Bridgett could imagine. "Yet you prevailed."

"We fell in love, married and had six kids."

Six. Not five. Maybe it was rude, but she had to ask. "You consider Cullen yours?"

Rachel stiffened. "Do you consider Robby yours?"

Okay, that was a mistake. "Yes."

"But…?" the older woman prodded.

Given permission to delve further, Bridgett asked, "Is there any difference in carrying a baby inside you and giving birth as opposed to simply being presented with a child, one day?"

Rachel relaxed. "None," she said gently. "If anything, sometimes I think I love Cullen more because of the shape he was in when he came to us at sixteen. He's still getting over the tumult of his early years." Her gaze narrowed. "How is he doing with all this?"

It was a lot, both women knew. To be publicly assumed

guilty of something you knew you hadn't done. Bridgett shrugged. She was close to Cullen and getting closer every day, but there was still a lot separating them, a lot he had yet to reveal. But what she did know, she liked, or maybe more to the point, loved. "He's mystified. Frustrated. A bit overwhelmed. More than anything, he wants to know the truth. Not just for himself, but for Robby."

Rachel sipped her tea. "Because he's sure his true parentage will be an issue in the future for Robby, like it was with him."

"Yes." And though Bridgett had told herself repeatedly it didn't matter, as long as Robby had a family who loved him, she worried about the ramifications of his never finding out where he came from or why he had been abandoned. That would be a lot to carry, and she didn't want Robby to suffer the way Cullen had.

"What about you?" Rachel asked gently. "Do you want to find this woman—or not?"

Bridgett bit her lip. "I'm not sure. Depends when you ask me. Sometimes I do, so I won't have this uncertainty hanging over us, and sometimes I don't because it could turn out that Robby has blood family who want him, and in court, biological ties trump all. Unless there's a concrete reason for them not to," she amended, "like addiction or abuse, and that would be a bad situation."

"I'm guessing Cullen is worried about what the social services and courts will eventually do, too."

Given how much he had bonded with baby Robby and Riot? Bridgett saw no reason not to admit it. "Yes, he is." She sighed and shook her head. "And then, on top of all that, having the potential buyers unexpectedly pull out of the auction..."

Rachel sat up straighter. "Wait. Could you repeat that?"

Briefly, Bridgett explained what had happened.

"Do you know which customers?" Rachel asked, brow furrowing.

"No."

"Or how many?"

"He said five this morning. There are still another fifteen bidding. At least, that was what he told me when he left earlier."

"That's good." Rachel finished her tea. She went for one last look at the sleeping baby, then tiptoed back out of the family room. "You'll call us if you need anything?" She stepped in to give Bridgett a hug.

Basking in the knowledge of what a wonderful mother Rachel was, Bridgett nodded. "I will."

WHEN CULLEN CAME in several hours later, she was gently dabbing baby oil onto Robby's scalp and working it through his silky dark curls.

Cullen sauntered closer, a bemused smile curving his sensual lips. He paused to greet her with a warm embrace, then bent down to kiss Robby, too. "Shouldn't you be using hair gel, instead of baby oil, if you want our boy to be all styling?"

Our boy. How nice that sounded, Bridgett thought wistfully. If only it were already true. She demonstrated with the oil-soaked cotton ball. "I'm softening the cradle cap on the top of his head."

"The…what?"

"See the little crust starting to form?" She pointed out the yellow skin. "Especially in the soft spot? This is cradle cap. Most new babies get it at some point during their first year."

"Should we be worried?" He went to the sink to wash up then ambled closer, still drying his hands on a paper towel.

"No." She used a soft-bristled baby brush to loosen the flakes, then combed them out of his hair.

He leaned in close, watching. "Are you just going to leave that in there?"

"No." She suddenly felt the overwhelming urge to kiss him again. "I'm going to wash it out while I give him his sponge bath. Want to help?"

His gave roved her upturned face before returning to her eyes. "You don't think I'll mess it up?"

"I won't let you mess it up," she promised with a smile.

"Okay then." He rolled up the sleeves on his shirt to above the elbow. "Let's do this."

Bridgett had already laid out a thick towel on the kitchen island. She settled Robby in the middle of it and poured a little warm water from the pitcher into a bowl. She added a squirt of soothing lavender-scented baby wash and, one hand still on Robby's chest to keep him from rolling off, dampened the washcloth.

"Wouldn't it be simpler to put him in a baby bath tub?"

Wanting Cullen to be as good at this as she was, she unsnapped the sleeper and removed Robby's damp diaper. "We will, as soon as the cord falls off."

Cullen watched as she quickly and methodically washed Robby thoroughly, from front to back. Then she swabbed the navel area with a small amount of rubbing alcohol, wrapped the infant in a towel and handed him to Cullen. "The shampoo is going to be a little trickier."

"What are we going to do?" he asked solemnly.

"You're going to hold him in your arms, yep, just like that, with his neck fully supported and his head slightly over the crook of your elbow. I'm going to dampen his hair with a little bit of water and then add some shampoo." She worked as she talked. "And then I'll lather his scalp."

The scent of lavender baby shampoo enveloped them.

Cullen made a funny face at their tiny charge and was rewarded with wide-eyed wonder. "He seems to like it," he reflected proudly.

"I think he likes being held."

Cullen chuckled and continued cuddling Robby tenderly. "Don't we all," he rumbled, just loud enough for her to hear.

His low, sexy voice generated a tsunami of need deep inside her. Not daring to look him in the eye, Bridgett *tsked*. "Okay, cowboy, let's stay on task."

"Hear that, Robby? Your mommy wants us to get serious here."

Mommy.

How she liked the sound of that.

Daddy, too.

Ignoring the way her nipples were tingling, Bridgett instructed casually, "If you sort of hold him over the basin, I'll rinse his head with the water in the pitcher. And then we'll be all done."

And, a minute later, they were.

Bridgett already had Robby's clothes all laid out, so she diapered him and put on a clean baby-blue sleeper. A matching knit cap went on his head. "Is there some reason you always have him wearing a hat?" Cullen asked when she gave him the baby to hold again.

"Newborn infants can get chilled easily. Covering their heads helps keep in the body heat."

"Ahhh."

It was hard to say who of the three of them was happier in that moment, as he moved in closer, so their sides were touching in an electrified line. Warmth exuded from the rock-hard muscles of his body. And she felt a melting sensation in her middle, completely at odds with the easy emotional territory she was attempting to stake out. She slanted Cullen a glance. Amazed at how at quickly and fiercely she had come to want him in her life. "We could get you and Riot matching caps, if you like."

He favored her with a sexy half smile, his eyes roving her face. "Actually, I think we should all wear matching caps." He bent over to kiss her temple. "One for all. All for one."

Another thrill swept through her. Were they about to take their relationship to another level? "Like the four musketeers," she surmised softly.

Cullen nodded, serious now. Then he paused, and turned so she could see Robby's face. "Hey, will you look at that?" he whispered, his brawny shoulder nudging hers slightly in the process. He looked as proud as any daddy in the newborn nursery. "The little cowpoke's asleep already."

"Bath time usually tuckers him out." Bridgett transferred him from Cullen's arms to his little bed, whispering, "We should put him down while he's still sleeping."

Cullen stood for one last long, tender look at the child they were quickly coming to think of as *their* son. "How long will he be out?"

"At least two hours." Riot, too, was passed out in his crate. "So, if you want, we can have a relaxing adults-only dinner."

Not a date.

But sort of like a date. Even though it would be experienced at home.

"Actually..." Cullen wrapped his hands around her waist, suddenly all hot, possessive male. "I had something much more pleasurable in mind."

Chapter Eleven

Bridgett saw the kiss coming and it was everything she had expected it would be. And everything she hadn't. It was soft and warm and unbearably seductive. Pure happiness soaring through her, she wound her arms about his neck and opened her mouth to the unerring pressure of his. Luxuriating in the scent of him, so brisk and familiar and masculine, she murmured, "I thought we were taking a break from this kind of intimacy."

He touched her cheek. "I wanted to give you a chance to reconsider, if that was what you wanted."

"Because of what Gavin implied during his third degree?" That Cullen was not to be trusted and did *not* have her best interests at heart, only his own?

"No, because of what I know to be true," Cullen corrected, stroking a hand through her hair. "That you're not, and never have been, a reckless person. Romantic? Hell, yes. Passionate in going after what you want? Absolutely. But the type to rush headfirst into anything? Especially with me...under these circumstances? No." He exhaled heavily, holding her gaze. "That's not you, Bridgett Monroe."

"Until now," Bridgett whispered, touched by his need to protect her, even as he let her know with a look and a touch and a kiss he still desired her. And when the time was right, intended to have her again.

Fortunately for the both of them, that time was tonight.

He held her by the shoulders as she rose on tiptoe and pressed her mouth to his, suggesting caution once again. "We can just hang out together, Bridgett. Make out a little."

"Oh, we'll do that all right," she promised, sliding her hands over the sinewy hardness of his chest. Pausing only to turn on the baby monitor, another gift, she took him by the hand and led him up the stairs, to the guest room, this time. "As well as so much more."

Determined to have all of him, she unbuttoned his shirt and pulled it off. Worked similar magic on his boots and pants. And, oops, there went his briefs, too.

"What's gotten into you?" he rasped, the twinkle in his navy blue eyes intensifying.

Enjoying what she was doing to him as much as he apparently liked her doing it, Bridgett sat back on the bed, admiring everything her quick work had uncovered. Glowing, golden skin. Smooth muscle. Enticing tufts of curly dark hair that spread across his chest and arrowed downward, delineating the goody trail. Nice broad shoulders. Not to mention long, powerful legs and strong arms.

She could sit here in front of him, just looking and admiring, all night long. As he noticed the depth of her enjoyment, his own pleasure grew.

Bridgett smiled, aware he was still waiting for her to reply. Her gaze shifted to his. "I made up my mind to stop putting off till tomorrow what I could enjoy right now. Tonight. And to that end…" She switched places with him, so he was on the bed. Still fully clothed herself, she dropped to her knees and captured the male essence of him with both hands, sculpting and caressing the hard, velvety-hot length.

"Whoa…" He groaned with arousal as she touched him with lips and tongue and teeth. "Getting a little ahead of you, here…"

No kidding, Bridgett thought. "That's okay," she breathed, as her nipples beaded and ached, and the damp throbbing between her legs intensified. She wanted to burn away the anxiety she felt over everything that might happen next. Concentrate on all that was good and right. And this, she thought on a blissful sigh, was the way to do it.

CULLEN HAD BEEN THINKING about making love to Bridgett again for days now. Because the problems that could keep them apart fell away when they were kissing and touching and driving each other wild and they were only dealing with what they wanted, what they felt.

And what he wanted most was her—in his home, in his bed, in his heart.

Not about to let her push him to the finish line without her, he curved his hands around her shoulders and drew her up to face him. "You, too," he said, undressing her, an item of clothing at a time. "I want to look at you."

Excitement building inside him, he stroked the silky texture of her skin, charting the hills and valleys as well as the plains in between. Her body shuddered beneath his questing fingertips, and he put all he wanted and needed, all he felt, into another searing kiss. He wanted to be everything to her, and he sensed, as he drew her down onto the bed, she wanted to be everything to him, too.

Feeling the yearning pouring out of her, he cupped the soft weight of her breasts in his hands and bent his head, loving her with his lips and mouth and tongue. She clung to him wordlessly, arching her back, opening herself up to him completely.

Shifting her onto her side, he pressed his body against hers, kissing her ceaselessly, until she was in a frenzy of wanting, her need making a low sound in the back of her throat. Until there was only the pulsing of her body, and his, only the wonder and affection in their hearts.

Her breath hitched as he found a condom and rolled it on. Her body trembled as he filled her. Yielding to him with the sweet surrender of a woman who was fated to be his, she clasped his shoulders as he kissed her and possessed her, again and again. Adrenaline rushed. Pleasure built and spiraled.

He slid his hands beneath her, lifting her, diving deep. Taking, as she gave, and giving her more in return. Until, together, they soared toward a completion more stunning and fulfilling than he had ever imagined possible.

And he knew this was what he wanted. Not just for now, but for all time.

"IT'S CRAZY," BRIDGETT SAID, as they snuggled together afterward, in no hurry to get up to eat dinner, "how much my life has changed in just a little over a week."

He loved the way she felt, holding him close, the silken warmth of her sprawled over his chest. "Mine, too." He ran a hand lovingly down her hip. "But there's no arguing that it's been for the better."

"For all of us." Bridgett smiled, and they made love again, slowly, thoroughly, tenderly this time, finishing just as Robby woke and started to fuss. Downstairs, Riot yelped from his crate, signaling he, too, needed attention.

Ready to tend to their more familial—but just as emotionally satisfying—duties, Cullen rose. "I'll put a bottle in the warmer, then feed Riot and take him out. Or…" He paused, thinking he might have assumed too much, taking charge so readily. "I could do the diaper." At least, he thought he could. "And you could do the other."

Looking tousled and well loved, she slipped into his shirt and headed for the stairs. "I like your first plan better."

Relieved, he winked. "Ah, teamwork. Nothing like it." He could help birth a calf blindfolded, but the fragility of a newborn infant still sometimes stymied him.

Riot was a little frisky after sleeping for so long, so Cullen snapped a leash on him and walked him down to the barn and back. When they walked in, he was disappointed to see Bridgett dressed in jeans, a T-shirt and bright blue moccasins. Her hair had been brushed into order and twisted atop her head, but there was no denying the flush in her cheeks or the plump kiss-swollen set of her lips.

"I kind of liked the way you looked in just my shirt."

She laughed, looking as contented as he felt. "If you behave, cowboy, you might be able to see me in it again before the night is through."

"Good." He ambled closer, drinking in the fresh lavender and baby powder scent of her. "'Cause I have plenty of them, you know. Dark denim, light blue denim, stone-washed denim…"

She mugged at him comically. "Tan and dark green canvas. And lots of blue chambray, too."

"Why, Ms. Bridgett…" He did his best imitation of a romantic comedy hero. "Have you been memorizing my wardrobe?"

Her eyes darkened affectionately. "Actually," she slid her hands up to his shoulders and rose on tiptoe, kissing him, "I might have been memorizing a lot of things about you."

They kissed again, but aware duties waited, reluctantly drew apart. "You must be starved," she murmured finally.

"You, too. And I am. But I need to do one thing first. Check my business email."

She stepped back, still studying him. "To make sure no one else has dropped out of the sale?"

"That. And…it's usual to have a lot of last-minute questions coming in."

Relaxing, she waved him on. "Go ahead then. I'll start warming up the dinner your stepmother brought for us."

Cullen nodded then paused in the doorway, memorizing that moment, savoring the sensation of just how happy he was. He had never imagined life on the ranch could be like this. Up until now, he had always felt there was something lacking. At first, a father of his own. Then, after his mother died, parents or family of any kind. After that gap had been filled, he'd lamented the lack of a woman he could keep company with and make love to. Now he had that, and all he wanted was for Bridgett and Robby and Riot to stay.

Even as the logical side of him knew they were living a fairy tale right now. That reality could come crashing down on all of them at any second. And if it did, Bridgett might not want anything further to do with him.

"Cullen?" she said softly, giving him an intent look. "Everything okay?"

He shook himself. "More than okay, darlin'," he promised. And right now, he told himself, he was good with that.

"GOOD NEWS, I take it?" Bridgett set the warmed food on the kitchen island. She took in the day's growth of beard and the flush of sun on his rugged, chiseled face. It seemed impossible he could appear even sexier now than when he'd been making love to her, but he did.

Cullen slipped onto a stool beside her, the happy gleam in his eyes at odds with his solemn tone. "Amazing, actually."

"Well, don't leave me in suspense! Tell me."

He handed her a serving bowl with exaggerated chivalry. "Two more local buyers dropped out."

She paused, a spoonful of mashed potatoes in mid-scoop. "And that's good?"

He flashed her a lopsided smile. "One of the biggest buyers in Nebraska—Dirk Cartwright of the Cartwright Ranch—has signed up to participate in the virtual auction in a big way."

She poured gravy over her potatoes. "Do you know Dirk?"

He nodded as they begin to serve themselves the pot roast. "They bought a few calves from me when I was living there. If I were to sell even a hundred Hotlander cattle to him, it would launch me into the big time."

"Congratulations."

He turned his gaze to hers. "Let's not get ahead of ourselves. This auction isn't over yet."

Bridgett tried not to read anything into the easy affection in his blue eyes, never mind how comfortable and intimate this all felt. "But if he did…"

His eyes glimmered. "It would mean I'd finally made Frank proud."

Bridgett ruminated on that. "He seems that way already."

Cullen made a seesawing motion, with his hand. "When he was my age, he already had ten thousand of the fifty thousand acres he owns now."

Bridgett looked at him. "You've mentioned that before.

Is that really what you want? That size ranch?" Because it could mean—would probably mean—leaving Laramie County, maybe even Texas.

He finished his string beans. "I'd be happy with that."

Would he? Bridgett studied him, her appetite suddenly fading. "But you want more?" she guessed.

For a moment she thought he wouldn't answer. That she'd delved into an area that was just too personal. Which sort of stung. She was beginning to think they had gotten to a point where there was nothing they couldn't share with each other.

His expression pensive, he turned to her, his knees brushing her thigh. "Have you always been a neonatal intensive care nurse?"

"No." Skin tingling, she swung around to face him. Now both their knees were touching. "I started in pediatrics."

He touched her hand, tracing each knuckle in turn. "Why did you move into N-ICU? Isn't it a lot harder, emotionally? Dealing with all those preemies, who might not make it?"

Bridgett inhaled, aware they were now traipsing into territory *she* might not want to discuss. Her appetite fading even more, she admitted, "It's very hard to take care of little ones who have so much stacked against them."

She paused, her lower lip quivering as she thought about the premature infants they'd lost over the years. With the rapid advances that had taken place in medicine, there weren't nearly so many tragic losses these days, but sometimes, a baby who had been getting better slowly, day by day, hour by hour, would suddenly take a turn for a worse. Their heart would fail. They'd stop breathing or develop an inoperable clot. And that was wrenching.

Not just for the family, but for all the doctors, nurses and support staff who worked tirelessly to help them thrive.

She clasped Cullen's hand tightly. "It's why I didn't think I could bear to foster a child not available for adoption." Her voice caught. "The thought of eventually having to let the child go, perhaps even returning to circumstances that were a lot less loving and stable than what I could offer, just slayed me."

"And yet you are." He gave her an admiring glance that meant more to her than any compliment she'd ever received.

"Because every instinct in me tells me that this is still our destiny. That I'm going to get to keep Robby and Riot. Otherwise, you're right." She inhaled a shuddering breath. "I never would have done this." *I never would have gotten to know you and fallen so hard and fast for you.*

Pausing, she sat back and withdrew her hand. "But what does my fostering to adopt have to do with the size of ranch you would like to have?"

Once again, she could see she had touched on something extremely personal.

He chose his words carefully. "Part of it is that the bigger the ranch and the bigger the herd, the more financial security I have." He went back to eating his dinner. "Given the way I grew up, with us moving every year or so, that was something in my early life that was sorely lacking."

She touched his arm. "I'm sorry you went through that."

He leaned down to kiss her fingers. "Hey, darlin', don't be. It's part of what nurtured my ambition." He straightened lazily so they could go back to eating. "The other reason I want to keep on expanding is that I'm easily bored."

She certainly didn't want him feeling that way!

"Building and improving my ranching operation is how I keep myself challenged, professionally." Half his mouth tilted in a sexy smile. "I like learning new things and putting that knowledge to use."

A thrill went through her as she thought about other ways that inclination could be put to use. "Hmm, learning new things," she echoed facetiously. "Putting that knowledge to use."

He ran his knee along the outside of her thigh. "You betcha."

She thrilled at the amorous look in his eyes. "Is it only on the ranch, cowboy?"

Already up off the stool, he mirrored her inviting tone. "How long do we have before we're back on baby and puppy duty?"

She took his hand. "A couple of hours."

He drew her to her feet. "Plenty of time for me to demonstrate just what an avid student I am."

Talk about a way to while away an evening! It was all she could do not to swoon. Bridgett wrapped her arms about his neck. "You think?"

Kissing her, he plucked her off her feet. "Let me show you."

THEY MADE LOVE AGAIN, took care of their little ones, slept, woke and then made love again just before dawn. They ate breakfast in shifts, between feeding, burping and cuddling Robby, and walking and feeding Riot. But it was okay; all the activity had a decidedly family feel to it.

At least, it did until Dan McCabe and Mitzy Martin showed up just as Cullen was about to head out to tend cattle with his hired hands.

Bridgett's heart sank in her chest. It was clear from the

looks on their faces they had news of some sort. Probably not good.

"I'm glad we caught you," Mitzy, who was in full social worker mode, said.

Dan's manner was official, as well. "We told you-all the sheriff's department would keep you updated, so we wanted to let you know we were able to get the rest of the photographs—the ones that remain unpublished—from the freelance photographer who took them."

Realizing she was the only adult in the room who wasn't up to speed on what was being discussed, Bridgett turned to Cullen. Matter-of-factly, he explained, "I went to the San Angelo newspaper earlier in the week. I thought they might have pictures from the high school career fairs that I attended there—that hadn't been printed in the newspapers. But when I explained to them why I wanted them, they said they would only speak to law enforcement or someone from social services."

"So Mitzy and I went over yesterday afternoon, talked to the freelance photographer hired to capture both events and explained the situation," Dan continued. "He understood we are doing our best to protect the privacy and health of the birth mother, and keep her from being spooked into running, assuming she already hasn't. He cooperated without a warrant. Gave me copies of every photo he took of Cullen speaking to the groups at both high schools."

"We're hoping you will recognize someone," Mitzy said.

There were some thirty black-and-white photographs in all. They spread them out over the kitchen island.

It didn't take long before Cullen identified a trio of students. "These three girls sitting in the front row. They were the ones quizzing me about ranch life and Riot Senior, and they also asked about my marital status and whether I thought I'd ever have a family someday, and so on."

Mitzy gaped in surprise. "That must have been some Q&A."

Cullen exhaled heavily. "Yeah. They were the final group I spoke to that day."

"You're sure this was them," Dan asked.

"Now that I see them again, absolutely." Cullen pointed to the girl in the middle. She was very tall and thin, and had long, curly dark hair, as thick and unruly as Robby's—and Cullen's, for that matter. She was wearing loose, unattractive clothing and had an intent, almost worried look on her face. "She seemed to be taking the lead. I remember thinking at one point that it was almost like she was interviewing me for a job."

"Maybe she was," Dan said with a beleaguered sigh, abruptly sounding more younger brother than deputy. "Like…adoptive daddy?"

"So you think…?" Bridgett pressed.

Cullen scrubbed a hand over his face. "Dan's right. This all fits. If it wasn't the dark-haired girl or one of her girlfriends who left the baby, they probably know who did."

"I can't believe we're going to have to wait until Monday to find out the identity of those students," Bridgett lamented when Mitzy and Dan had left, promising to call as soon as they had more news on the baby-mama front. "That's three whole days of wondering and worrying!"

"Maybe it's a good thing. The virtual auction is tomorrow."

Saturday morning.

Cullen continued, "I'd prefer the sale be over with before we have to deal with whatever is coming next."

He had a point there, Bridgett conceded. It would be awful to be getting news regarding Robby's biological mother in the midst of the most important business transaction of Cullen's fiscal year. And there was something else…

Drawing a deep breath, she moved closer. "Why didn't you tell me about any of this?"

Cullen shrugged, to her deep disappointment, once again shutting her out. "I didn't want you to worry about something that might not yield anything. As it initially didn't. You had enough to deal with between the mortgage and the baby and trying to get chosen to foster-adopt." His eyes gleamed. "I was trying to protect you. It's what a man does for his woman."

His woman. Bridgett gulped. "You're saying…?"

"That you're my woman? Hell, yes. What did you think? That this was casual for me? It's not, Bridgett. It never has been." His eyes closed to half-mast. "It never will be." Slowly, he lowered his head and cradled her face in his big, rough hands.

"For me, either," Bridgett whispered back, her heart pounding in her chest.

The raw affection in his embrace made her catch her breath. This time there was nothing easy about his kiss. It was hot, persuasive, hungry. She kissed him back, in much the same way, knowing that, once the sale was over the next morning, they would have the rest of the weekend to enjoy. But would it be their last—as the makeshift family neither she nor Cullen had ever imagined would come about?

Bridgett didn't know.

Wasn't sure she *wanted* to know.

Fiercely, she splayed her hands over the hardness of

his chest and drew back. "That was a pretty passionate sentiment, cowboy."

He ran a hand down her spine, positioning her even more securely against him. "You got that, right, sweetheart."

She sighed blissfully, luxuriating in his heat and his strength. "And here I thought you didn't have a romantic bone in your body."

"I never thought I did." Confident as ever, he ran his hands through her hair and kissed her again, even more thoroughly this time. "Until you showed me otherwise."

Chapter Twelve

"Three minutes!" Bridgett exclaimed in stunned amazement Saturday morning. It seemed like he had just gone into his home office to monitor the virtual auction, and now he was telling her it was over?

"I got top dollar," Cullen told her proudly. "Way more than I expected."

"Who-all bought them?" Bridgett continued folding laundry.

"The Cartwright Ranch."

"That big outfit in Nebraska?"

Cullen nodded. "Dirk outbid everyone, pushed the price up to a level none of the Texas ranchers could compete with."

Bridgett stood and threw her arms around his neck. "Congratulations."

Grinning, he hugged her back. "Thanks."

"Is it always so fast?"

He joined her on the sofa. "The process has been getting speedier. The first time I did this, it took most of the day to sell them all. Last year, it took me about an hour to sell the entire group."

She took the cell phone out of her hip pocket. "We should call your folks."

His hand covered hers. "Why?"

Stunned by his reluctance, when just seconds before he had been bursting with joy, she turned her palm up to clasp his and tried again. "We should let them know you had a record sale. Heck, we should invite them all over. Have a party to celebrate."

His dark eyes shuttered. He stood and walked away. "Ah, I don't think so."

She followed him into the kitchen. "Why not?" She knew for a fact that the McCabe clan was as big as the Monroe's on family gatherings.

He shrugged and pulled a jug of orange juice out of the fridge. "I just don't think it's a good idea."

Still puzzling over his attitude, she moved closer. "Do you think they won't be happy for you?"

"No." He poured two glasses, recapped the bottle and set it back in the fridge, his expression as careful as his words. "They will be."

O-kay. She lounged with her back against the island, accepting the glass he gave her. Stymied, she studied him over the rim. "Do you think they will expect that you should have gotten a higher return?"

He downed his drink in one long thirsty draught. Set it aside. "Hell, no. What I got was damn near amazing," he stated firmly. "More than I ever could have anticipated."

"Then what is it?" she asked softly, needing and wanting to understand him. "What's keeping you from wanting to share this very good news with your family?"

"I just think it might be something better done a few weeks from now."

His tone was so vague. "This has something to do with the implied accusation against you, doesn't it?"

"You're right." His lips took on a determined slant. "I'll feel a lot more comfortable facing my family after my name is cleared."

She tried not to notice how handsome he was in a new pair of jeans and canvas shirt that brought out the navy in his eyes. He had also shaved closely that morning. "I think you're underestimating them."

He sighed and sent her a piercing glance. "I think you're underestimating how much I want to enjoy our time together." His eyes met and held hers. "So, what do you say," he drawled, "we focus on that and forget everything else—especially business—for the rest of the day?"

AN HOUR LATER, the four of them were enjoying a picnic lunch at the Triple Canyon. "So this is where you had your family parties, growing up?"

There were several picnic tables and an open air pavilion at the end of a gravel lane, high atop a rocky ridge. The area was windy and cool, and had a spectacular view of the rocky canyons, wildflower meadows and winding streams that comprised the thousand-acre ranch.

"Except," Bridgett pointed out, "we didn't have the wind turbines along the fence line then."

"It's beautiful."

"And private."

"The little ones like it." Robby was in a BabyBjorn. He had just finished his bottle and was happily nestled against the solid warmth of Cullen's chest. Riot was leashed to one of the tables in the center of the pavilion and was alternately chewing on a couple of dog toys, watching the two of them and looking out onto the amazing vista beyond.

"We all still come here a lot." Bridgett doled out the grilled chicken sandwiches, chips and fruit they'd hastily packed. "Sometimes as a group, sometimes individually."

"I can see why." He uncapped a thermos of hot coffee. "It's a great place for a picnic."

"Especially on a day like today." When they had so much to celebrate, so much at risk…

They lingered over their meal, talking about matters big and small. Finally, Cullen said, "Want to take a selfie, for Robby's baby book?"

Not too long ago, he'd been warning her against getting prematurely attached. Now—to the immense surprise of both of them—his heart was in play, too.

Bridgett smiled. "Why not? I definitely want to remember this."

Bridgett set Riot on her lap. Cullen turned sideways, so they could see the profile of Robby in his BabyBjorn, sleeping with his head resting on Cullen's chest. They put their heads together, and with his arm outstretched, he took the picture with his phone.

"One more…"

They grinned. Riot—impatient now—let out a happy bark.

Together, they walked the area around the pavilion, found a field of bluebonnets, and—like every other young family in Texas that time of year—took another couple of selfies against a backdrop of wildflowers.

"Speaking of photos," Cullen remarked as they headed back up to the picnic pavilion. "You were going to show me your childhood photos."

"My albums are back at the ranch house, but I've got some of them on my social media pages." She accessed them on her phone.

He studied the photo of her mom, dad and all her siblings. It was the last photo taken of all of them together.

Cullen studied the picture with a wistful gaze. "You look like you were a happy family."

Bridgett nodded, poignant emotion filling her heart as Cullen transferred Robby and the BabyBjorn to her and they settled at a picnic table once again. "We were, until my mom and dad died suddenly in a car crash, and then it was sad chaos for a long time afterward."

He wrapped his arm around her shoulders and brought her—and Robby—into the curve of his body. "How come?"

"My older sister, Erin, was married with three small children. G.W., her husband at the time, was a geologist for an oil company and traveled constantly. My older brother—grumpy old Gavin—was in med school, so he wasn't around a lot to help out."

"Sounds…stressful."

"It was. We sold all the cattle my dad had been running on the ranch. But we still had the Western-wear store in town—Monroe's—that had been in our family for generation to run. So Erin was managing that and the custom boot-making business that went along with it."

"Sounds even harder."

"Then her daughter, Angelica, got seriously ill. G.W. couldn't handle it and checked out. Literally and figuratively. Two years later, when Angelica died at just six, they divorced. Meanwhile, Erin was raising Bess and me, and even though we were teens at the time, we tried to do everything we could to pitch in to help out around the house and also help her look after our baby brother, Nick, who was only ten when our parents passed."

"Sounds unimaginably rough."

"It was. Anyway, we stopped taking group photos after my parents died because it was so hard anyway, without Mom and Dad, and doing that just made us miss them more acutely. So, suffice it to say, there's a big gap in my family photo history. But…" She brightened, glad to have of it all out there, at long last. "I do have these pictures from nursing school."

She thumbed through a couple of dozen pictures on her phone. "I still didn't really want to memorialize anything, but my fellow nursing students took photos of me whether I wanted them to or not, so there are a fair number of them. Including a lot of me and Bess."

"Does this have anything to do with why you resisted getting married right out of college?"

"Ah, perceptive, cowboy."

He waited. Sensing there was more.

She knew that as long as she was baring her soul, she might as well tell him everything—the good, the bad and the ugly. "Yeah. In retrospect, I know it's selfish, but back then, all I could think was that when my parents passed I was just at the age where I would have started dating, and I had to step in and help Erin out with chores and babysitting her kids as well as my younger brother."

She let it all out in a rush, as her emotions soared out of control. "And then there wasn't enough money, and we all had to put ourselves through college, so Bess and I were always working and going to school, and I felt like I never got the freedom to go out and have fun and do as I please like most of my peers."

"Anyone in your position would have felt the same way, sweetheart," he said softly.

"Maybe, maybe not," she acknowledged. "Anyway…" She stopped and shook her head, comforted by the depth of understanding in Cullen's mesmerizing blue eyes. "The thought of marrying someone I wasn't sure I felt deeply enough about to make a lifelong commitment to….and having a ton of kids right away…seemed like a death sentence."

"Interesting." He tugged tenderly on a lock of her hair. "When you talked about your ex before, you didn't say you didn't love him."

And she hadn't, for a very good reason. Bridgett gathered her courage and looked deep into Cullen's eyes. "That was because I didn't know what life-changing love was then." *I hadn't found Robby or Riot or spent time with you.* "I know now."

IT WAS CULLEN'S turn to feel trapped. Not by all that he felt about Bridgett—which he welcomed—but by what he couldn't say just yet.

Not without rushing her into something neither of them was quite ready for. Especially with so much still unresolved. "I'm sorry that you had such a hard time." He leaned down to buss her temple.

She turned slightly and kissed the underside of his jaw. "Right back at you, cowboy." She sighed, still snuggling close, and glanced up at him wryly. "Sounds like the high school years were not particularly good for either of us."

"Maybe it will be different for Robby." He hoped.

Bridgett smiled.

Cullen's phone chimed with a text message from Frank McCabe. Great news on the auction! You've got everyone buzzing. Want to get together to celebrate?

Cullen paused, then punched in a return message. Sounds good. Couple weeks?

A long pause. Let us know where and when.

Bridgett read the exchange. "That was nice."

Cullen nodded, his expression inscrutable.

She studied him, perplexed, able to feel the wall around his heart going back up. "You don't think it was sincere?" she asked.

"It was."

"Then what's the problem…?"

He shrugged and put his phone away. "Things have just never been that comfortable between us."

"Maybe if you tried harder?" she suggested gently. "Went through that door that he just opened for you?"

Clenching his jaw, Cullen gazed out at the canyons, and Bridgett had never felt more removed from him. She curved her fingers around his forearm. "Look, I know it's none of my business," she pushed on with difficulty. "I just know that if I had another day or hour or minute with my folks, I wouldn't waste it. I'd embrace it with everything I had."

Another terse nod in response.

She could tell by the way he was still studying the wind farm in the distant part of the ranch that he thought she didn't—couldn't—understand.

And maybe she didn't.

Maybe, ever the sentimental fool, she was only seeing what she wanted to see. Not what really was, between him and the McCabes.

One thing was for certain, he did not appreciate what she had said, no matter how well-intentioned it had been.

CULLEN WAS RELIEVED when Bridgett let the subject of his family drop and spent the rest of the day going back to their original plan—which was to celebrate his big win. And it *was* a huge success.

So much so that he felt he might finally be in a financial position to think about settling down. Getting married. Having a family. And there was only one woman he had in mind for that course of action.

Aware it was way too soon to be thinking or talking that way, however, he concentrated on having fun. They went into town for dinner and ate at one of the outside tables along the sidewalk so that Robby could hang out in his stroller while a leashed Riot lounged at their feet.

The next day, however, work called. He had 500 head

of cattle that had been sold to be separated into smaller, manageable groups and moved to pastures closer to ranch roads.

He came in at dark that evening, exhausted, and was welcomed with a nice hot dinner that Bridgett had made. A nighttime walk with Riot and cuddling with Robby followed that, and bedtime meant sweet and tender love-making with Bridgett.

The next morning brought more of the same.

He paused before heading out. Bridgett looked gorgeous, her hair all tousled, cheeks still pink with sleep. "You going to be okay alone today?"

She smiled, amused. "I think I can manage, cowboy."

"Mitzy…Dan…the search."

She heaved a big sigh. "I haven't forgotten it's Monday and they are headed to the high school to try and identify the three girls. I've just been trying not to think about it."

"Good plan."

She looked so vulnerable.

"You know, you could always call in reinforcements for Riot and Robby, and saddle up."

She wrinkled her nose. "What makes you think I know how to herd cattle?"

"You said your dad raised cattle until you were fourteen…"

"Fine. So I might know a thing or two about herding. And your point is?"

"Thought you might enjoy a change of scenery." He sat down on the edge of the bed and enveloped her in a hug. Anything to keep her from worrying too much.

She splayed her hands across his chest. Her eyes were all soft and misty. "Maybe one day," she promised softly. "Today, I'm going to be all mom."

He couldn't blame her for wanting to cherish every

second. "I'll have my cell phone with me. If you hear anything…"

"I'll call. Promise."

He brought her close for another hug. He breathed in the womanly scent of her. "You're going to get the family you want, sweetheart."

She drew back, her lower lip quivering, no longer the ultraconfident Bridgett he'd clashed with in the hospital nursery. "How do you know?" she whispered.

Easy. He buried his face in the fragrant softness of her hair. "Because I am personally going to see to it."

One way or another she would have a baby and puppy to love, a husband who cherished her, and a place for them all to call home.

And when that happened, they would both know what true contentment was.

FOR BRIDGETT, THE day went on forever. She hated when life spiraled out of her control. The way it had when her parents died. The way it was now. The only help for that was activity focused on someone else.

And that someone was Cullen.

He had done so much for her and Robby and Riot.

Been so kind and selfless and downright heroic.

She knew she owed him, big time. She also realized there was one thing she could do for him, and she hoped that would be just as meaningful. So she worked on arranging it all day long, via phone calls, texts and emails. And by late afternoon her big thank-you to him was all set.

And still there was no word from the sheriff's department or social services.

Finally, just as Cullen was coming in from the range at five in the evening, Mitzy stopped by. The social worker looked as frustrated as Bridgett felt. "No news?" she guessed.

Mitzy set her bag down. "We were able to ID all three girls. Sherri and Dawn are still students at the high school in San Angelo. The tall one—with the dark curly hair, Marie Griffin—dropped out in January, said she hadn't been getting along with her parents and was going off to live with her grandmother in Tulsa."

"And…?"

"Dan checked. Her grandmother died last summer."

Bridgett's heart lurched in her chest. "So, where is she?"

Cullen moved in, simultaneously taking her hand and pushing her onto the closest seat—a kitchen stool.

The social worker frowned. "We don't know. Dan's trying to track Mr. and Mrs. Griffin down now. I got their phone numbers from the school, too. We're both leaving messages all over the place. If we don't have any luck, we'll ask the two other girls, but records show they have been in school with only a couple intermittent absences, due to illness, this semester, so I'm not sure if they will be able to tell us anything or not."

"Do school officials think Marie Griffin might have been pregnant?" Cullen asked.

"The guidance counselor wasn't sure. She just recalled her looking both stressed and relieved the day Marie came in to say she was leaving."

"The time frame fits," Cullen said.

Mitzy nodded. "It does. Although no one at the school recalls Marie dating anyone there. She was a pretty quiet seventeen-year-old. Actually, she's eighteen now. She had a birthday last month."

"So now what?" Bridgett asked, beginning to feel her life spiraling out of control again.

Mitzy sighed. "We let Dan do his job. I'll do mine. As soon as we learn anything else, we'll contact you. In the meantime, stay put. Stay calm. And Bridgett?" She paused, beaming her approval. "The new plan for your living arrangements is likely to go over *much better* with the department heads at DCFS and the family court judge."

Chapter Thirteen

New plan? What new plan? Cullen wondered. He stayed inside with Robby and Riot while Bridgett walked the social worker out. When she came back in, he noticed her face was flushed with emotion. He didn't know whether to feel concerned for her welfare or betrayed. The truth was, he felt a little of both. "What was Mitzy talking about?"

"You know I have my meeting with the social services department on Thursday afternoon, to talk about Robby's placement." Bridgett was chipper, as always, when things were going her way.

"I knew it was this week. I don't think you had told me when, though."

In the laundry room, the washer dinged, signaling the cycle had finished. She spun around and headed for the small space, leaving him to follow. "Well, it could still be moved up or back, depending on what happens with Marie Griffin, and so on. But I was only initially allowed to foster Robby because his health was uncertain and I was an approved foster mother who was also a registered nurse, and an N-ICU, one at that."

He lounged against the door, giving her room to work. "I remember."

"Luckily, Robby has been healthy."

He let his gaze rove from the satisfied curve of her

soft lips to her sparkling green eyes. "His umbilical cord hasn't fallen off yet."

"Actually, it did. This morning. In his diaper."

Aware she was awaiting his reaction to such momentous new parent news, he said, "Oh."

"So…" Bridgett bent to take the clothes from the dryer and drop them into an empty laundry basket "…from the standpoint of his health, anyway, there is no more reason why he would need to be placed with me, specifically."

He tore his eyes from the enticing way her knee-length cotton skirt hugged her slender hips and her cotton blouse her breasts as she moved the damp baby clothes from washer to dryer.

"Except he loves you and is used to you, and I'm damn sure, thinks of you as his mommy."

"And you his daddy." She shut the door and leaned across the top of the machine to set the dials and switch it on. Swinging back to him, she leaned up against the machine, her hands braced on either side of her. "But we both know that could—maybe will—change." Her mouth took on a sober line.

A tense silence fell.

"What does Mitzy have to say about all this?"

"She's going to support me in my request to continue beyond the approved two-week period and foster-adopt," she informed him. "But I need to have all my ducks in a row. Including and especially the housing issue."

"I told you. You can continue to stay here as long as you like. You all can."

Briefly, gratitude shone in her eyes. "I know." Her soft lips took on a new, troubled slant. "But…Mitzy feels that because you and I have no longstanding commitment to each, other than the one we have forged the last twelve days or so, coupled with the fact that I have decided to take a full maternity leave from the hospital…and lost the house I was applying for a mortgage for…that I need to have a more solid housing plan in place."

"And now you have one?" he asked, with a great deal more equanimity than he felt.

"Yes, we do," she answered with a nod. "My twin, Bess, and I are going to buy a house together. We were both planning on purchasing our own homes, individually, but we could just as easily pool our funds and buy a bigger place to accommodate all of us right now. And we could stagger our work schedules so that there would always be one of us there for Robby. Hence, he wouldn't need to go into day care at all!"

It was a great solution. One DCFS would have trouble finding fault in. The only one not served well by it was him. He swallowed his hurt and anger and forced himself to be the Texas gentleman he had been raised to be. "How long is all that going to take?"

"Well, that's the rub." Reaching up, Bridgett undid the clasp holding her hair up on the back of her head. She clipped it to the open neckline of her blouse. "Bess and I haven't started looking yet, and we'd have to find a place and go through the whole mortgage process."

With a beleaguered sigh, she ran her fingers through the silky strands, combing them into place. "So, in the interim, Robby and Riot and I would need a place to stay."

She retwisted her hair and knotted it on the back of her head again. "Nick and Sage have invited us to bunk with them at the Triple Canyon as soon as the remodeling is complete, in another month. In the meantime…"

Her eyes lifted to his and a muscle ticked in his jaw as he listened in silence.

"…Sage's mother, Lucille Lockhart, has said we could all move out to the guest quarters on her Circle H ranch—

a six bath, six bedroom bunkhouse with full kitchen and living area. As well as staff at our disposable, should we need it."

She sounded really happy and relieved about all of this. Which begged the question—did she really not know how bereft the new arrangement would leave him?

He forced himself to do what she was doing, and focus on the welfare of their two little charges. "Seems like you have it all figured out."

She studied him, intuitive as always. "You're upset. Or maybe insulted?"

He definitely felt burned by the way she had left him out of the equation. No question. Although maybe he shouldn't. She'd made it clear from the start that her fling with him, as well as her lodging here, was only a temporary solution to a very long-term problem.

She caught his hand in hers. "Please tell me what's on your mind."

The feel of her smooth skin touching his brought only partial comfort. He shrugged and tried to summon up what little gallantry he seemed to have left. "I'm just wondering if I should read anything into this."

She blinked. "What do you mean?"

With a disgruntled frown, he stepped back. "It's interesting that you will buy a property with your sister, but not allow me to buy you the house that you wanted in town, and rent it back to you, thereby eliminating all these complicated financial and domestic arrangements." *That are going to take you and Riot and Robby away from the Western Cross and away from me.*

She leaned back against the washer and looked up at him. "It's not the help I'm rejecting. It's the way it might look to outsiders."

Unsure what she meant, he waited.

"I guess if we are able to locate the biological mother and get proof the baby isn't yours, then that part of the scandal goes away and anything you do would be viewed as noble. If we don't…" She flushed and shook her head in silent remonstration. "Then, as you said, people are always going to wonder."

Reluctantly, he had to admit to himself that she had a point.

"And if you buy a home to house the kid—and his caretaker—in, people will *really* wonder. It will fuel the talk. It'll hurt your reputation. And my chances to foster-adopt."

Unfortunately, Cullen had to admit, that was true, too.

Her eyes shone. "It will also make it look like I can't do this as a single parent." Her low tone took on a defiant edge. "When we both know I can. I just need a little help to get started, since this was all so sudden. And my family, the whole Monroe clan, and even Lucille Lockhart—my brother's mother-in-law—will be here to back me up. Now and in the future. You yourself have promised me the same."

He certainly had.

Glad she had taken his offer to heart, he listened quietly as she continued.

"As you pointed out, that is a very powerful statement to make on my behalf. Mitzy agrees. She thinks her supervisors and the family court judge will, too. In fact, with this new plan and all the concrete ways my siblings have vowed to help me, she thinks I now have a real shot to foster-adopt Robby."

Cullen could see how much this meant to her.

Worse, he felt like the world's biggest jackass for making this more about him and their new romance than the two little ones they should be looking out for.

"Of course, it goes without saying—" Bridgett choked up "—I want you to be a part of our lives, even after we move out." She waved a hasty hand, amending in a low, strangled voice. "If that's what you want, of course."

He took her in his arms, holding her close. "Of course it's what I want, sweetheart." He buried his face in the intoxicating lavender fragrance of her hair. "Never ever doubt that, okay?"

"O-kay." She sniffled. "I'm sorry I didn't tell you. I just..." She gulped and went on, voice even more wobbly. "I wasn't sure how you'd take it."

He drew back. "Badly?"

She laughed, as he meant her to. But her smile trembled as tears glistened in her eyes.

And suddenly he knew her moving out was going to be every bit as difficult for her as it was for him. "I'll miss you," he rasped. "When you go." *If you go.* He was still working on a plan to keep her here. And not just temporarily.

"I'll miss you, too." She hugged him back.

He lowered his head and delivered a tender kiss. "But let's not get ahead of ourselves here. You-all aren't gone yet."

That night, after they put the little ones to bed, they made love again. He laid claim to her lips and body as he wanted to lay claim to her heart and soul. And this time, when they came together in shattering sensation, he knew—even if she didn't, yet—that there was no going back for either of them. She belonged to him, and he to her, and that was the way it was always going to be. Together, they would have the passionate relationship and family they had both always wanted. Whether she—and Robby and Riot—moved out temporarily or not.

BRIDGETT HAD KNOWN that Cullen wouldn't be happy about her news. She had also known he was practical enough to understand why she had to lean on her family more than him right now.

The sexy, tender way he'd made love to her the night before had proved it.

She'd returned the gesture by putting all the hope she felt for their future into her lovemaking, too. Hence, they both woke up in a fine mood. Which was a good thing. Tuesday was going to be a big day. "The trucks are here." Bridgett marveled at the sight shortly after dawn.

One after another, the cattle haulers and Cartwright Ranch trucks rumbled up the road.

His expression now all business, Cullen watched a late model luxury pickup park close to the ranch house. "And so is Dirk Cartwright." He grabbed his hat from the hook by the door and settled it on his head.

Bridgett resisted the urge to kiss Cullen goodbye, the way a wife did when she sent her husband off to work, and contented herself with one last long look, instead. "I didn't realize he was coming here, too." She followed him to the door.

"A purchase this big?" Cullen flashed a smile. He bent his head and briefly captured her lips. "He's going to want to check on the herd in person."

While Bridgett and the baby watched from the window, Cullen met the snowy-haired rancher outside. The hardy six-foot cattleman vigorously shook Cullen's hand. The two set off.

All morning long, both the Western Cross and Cartwright Ranch crews worked fiercely. One by one the big semi cattle haulers and the Cartwright Ranch pickup trucks drove away.

At one point, the two men left, too.

When Cullen returned, he was alone and looking a little shell-shocked. Bridgett met him at the door. "Are you okay?"

Noting all was quiet, Cullen took her by the hand and led her back onto the front porch so they could talk. "Dirk Cartwright made me an incredible, unexpected offer. He wants to sell me the Cartwright Ranch."

Bridgett did a double take. "In Nebraska?"

Cullen nodded and sat down the steps, overlooking the ranch. "Sixty-five thousand acres. Five thousand head of cattle."

Bridgett settled beside him. "That's more than your dad has, isn't it?"

He nodded.

She turned slightly to face him, her bent knee nudging his muscular thigh. "Can you afford it?"

He grinned. "Here's the miraculous part." He leaned forward in a confidence-inspiring pose, forearms on his thighs. "Dirk Cartwright wants me to move there *now* and begin managing the operation. And buy in incrementally, year by year, until I own it all a decade from now."

A front was moving in, turning the late-afternoon sky a dark blue-gray. Bridgett shivered in the newly cool air. "You'd sell the place here?"

Cullen nodded, seeming oblivious to the damp, chilly air. "I'd have to. But it wouldn't be a problem. Jeanne Phipps has told me more than once she could sell any property I renovate."

Bridgett folded her arms in front of her to cover up the pearling of her nipples and wished she'd thought to put on a sweater. "You wouldn't flip the Cartwright place?"

"No." His voice was casual. "It's state-of-the-art already. I'd probably change the name once I owned it, though."

Her heart skidded to a halt, then took up an erratic beat. She perched on the edge of the top step. "So, are you going to take him up on his offer?"

Even though he had just been talking like the decision were already made—at least on some level—Cullen seemed brought up short by her assumption. He turned to her, dark brow furrowed. "I don't know. I can barely wrap my head around it right now." He paused to study her in concern. "This upsets you?"

What could she say to that that would be true and wouldn't hurt him? After all, he had supported her through so much, worked side by side with her to see she achieved her dreams. Which, even now, weren't quite within reach. Even if they soon would be.

Scolding herself for her selfishness, she straightened. "No, of course not. I'm proud of you, Cullen."

And she was. She was just sad for herself. Because once again, she was involved with a man who had dreams that were right for him and not for her. She feigned an enthusiasm she couldn't begin to feel. "How long do you have?" she asked brightly.

"Dirk Cartwright told me to take a couple of weeks to think about it." He shook his head. "I don't think it will take that long to make a decision, though."

Bridgett knew what she hoped it would be.

The phone rang. He looked at his caller ID. "It's Dan." He picked up and put the call on speakerphone so Bridgett could hear. "Hey, little brother. Got some news for us?"

"As a matter of fact," Dan said gruffly, his voice coming out loud and clear, "I do. We still haven't been able to locate either Marie Griffin or her parents but we *did* talk to the neighbors at their home in San Angelo."

Bridgett tensed.

Cullen put his arm around her.

"And?" he prodded.

Dan continued, "They said Mr. and Mrs. Griffin aren't exactly model parents. In fact, they've complained for years about how the burden of having a child in their teens cramped their style. When they came into a small inheritance late last fall, they quit their jobs and put their home on the market. It sold around Valentine's Day. They stored what few belongings they decided to keep, then took off to backpack across every mountain range in America."

Cullen asked, "Did their daughter go with them?"

"No. According to her parents, she took off in January to start living her own life. Which they had expected her to do, anyway, as soon as she was eighteen. The fact she left a little earlier than that was not a surprise to her folks. They said she was always independent to a fault."

"Independent or neglected?" Bridgett murmured.

Dan exhaled. "From the sound of it, a little of both. Anyway, no one has seen any of the Griffins in several months. Although we do have the parents' cell phone numbers and we are still trying to get in touch with them."

"What about Marie?" Cullen asked. "Does she have a cell phone?"

Dan exhaled. "No one knows. What they do know is that the parents refused to pay for one. Said whatever Marie had, she had to earn."

"So we still have no idea where Marie is?" Cullen asked, sounding impatient once again.

"None. We had the school guidance counselor call in her friends, Sherri and Dawn, today. She asked them if they had any info on their friend. They both said no."

Noting how nervous Bridgett was getting, Cullen wrapped his arm even more tightly about her shoulders. "Did the counselor believe them?" he asked.

Dan scoffed. "Not for a red-hot minute. So Mitzy and

I are going to the school to talk to them tomorrow afternoon. The school asked that their parents be there, too, so that was as soon as we could arrange it."

"You'll let us know?"

"We will." Dan paused. "And since Bridgett is there with you, on to a more cheerful note—when is the party starting?"

Chapter Fourteen

"Party?" Cullen rolled to his feet as a bevy of vehicles came down the lane.

"Actually…" Bridgett winced, standing, too, and wishing she'd had a moment to prepare Cullen for the celebration she had planned. "The McCabes are already arriving en masse." It was Cullen she hadn't exactly expected to be here yet.

"Great! Be there in fifteen."

Cullen turned to her, an unreadable expression on his face. Without warning, they were back to the first day in the hospital corridor with him not trusting her one bit. "Bridgett? What's going on?" he ground out.

Too late, she realized she'd made a huge mistake. "Surprise!" she said weakly.

He wheeled around and strode across the porch and back into the ranch house. Fury emanated from every pore. "Who-all did you invite?"

She struggled to keep up with him. "Frank and Rachel. Your five siblings."

He drummed his fingers on the kitchen island. "Anyone else?"

"Ah…no." She hadn't been quite sure how this was going to go, so she hadn't wanted an audience if it turned out to be unbearably awkward.

He exhaled heavily. Abruptly looking as if he had the whole world on his shoulders. "I wish you hadn't done this," he said.

Right now, so did she. "Too late," she offered brightly, as Robby, alert to the new tension in the ranch house, began to fuss. Bridgett went to get the baby. Riot, who'd been sleeping on his cushion, got up, went into the very back of his crate and settled there, watchful.

Rachel and Frank came through the back door, bearing food and beverages. "Congratulations!" Rachel said, stopping to kiss Cullen on the cheek. "We're so glad you agreed to have a party now!"

Except he hadn't agreed, Bridgett thought, observing her lover's smile. He hadn't known anything about it. And clearly would have vetoed it wholeheartedly if he had.

Rachel set cellophane-covered trays of oven-ready enchiladas down. She turned back to Cullen to give him another big hug. "We are so proud of you! Selling out the entire group in three minutes!"

Finally, Cullen began to relax. He couldn't help but smile at his stepmother's warm approval. "It was something, all right."

"A record for the Western Cross!" Frank stepped up to shake his eldest son's hand.

Matt McCabe came in. The military vet had been uncharacteristically joyless since returning from Afghanistan several months prior. Still, he managed a respectful smile as he put down the beer and sodas he carried and strode over to give Cullen a high five. "Way to go, man."

"Thanks," Cullen said.

Jack McCabe came in, carrying big take-out containers of Mexican rice and beans. The orthopedic surgeon had his two-, three- and four-year-old daughters—and their fifty-year-old nanny—in tow. Tragically widowed almost two years ago, he was being chased by hordes of women but had vowed far and wide to remain single for the rest of his life.

He set the offerings on the counter, next to the enchiladas, held out his hand to Cullen. "You've got my respect, brother."

Cullen nodded. He dipped his head toward Jack's brood. "Right back at you."

Businessman Chase McCabe came in, carrying a brand-new fine leather saddle from his manufacturing firm in one hand and a boxed cake in the other. He set the cake down and handed the saddle to Cullen. "Proud of you, man. And now that you're such a big shot, maybe you could test this out for me and let me know what you think."

"Thanks." Cullen shook his hand, practically beaming now. "I will."

Beginning to relax—it looked like this hastily arranged family get-together might work out, after all—Bridgett grinned, too.

Cullen's baby sister, Lulu McCabe, breezed through the door carrying a big bag of fresh flour tortillas from the Mexican bakery in town and a bottle of honey from her own hives. She set both down on the counter, then turned to hug Cullen and offer her congratulations. "And to celebrate," she finished happily, "I've got everything we need for sopaipillas!"

Last but not least, Dan came in, still in his sheriff's deputy uniform, carrying a big bag of freshly made restaurant tortilla chips and salsas. "Way to go!" He took Cullen by the shoulder, brought him in close and shook his hand. "You've turned Western Cross into one fine ranch, brother!"

Unable to keep quiet any longer, Bridgett burst in, "You

don't know the half of it! You should hear about the offer he just got!"

Thunderstruck, Cullen turned to her.

"What?" Rachel buzzed, excited, too.

Cullen seemed at a loss as to how to begin to tell them. Bridgett helped him along. "Dirk Cartwright was just here. He offered Cullen a stake in his Nebraska ranch."

The only one in the room who did not look surprised by the revelation was Frank McCabe. "What kind of stake?" his father asked.

Briefly, Cullen explained what he had already told Bridgett. With a lot less enthusiasm this time.

"So, you'd have to pull up stakes and leave here?" Rachel asked, clearly upset by the notion.

Her husband turned to her. "It's an offer of a lifetime, honey. I think he has to at least consider it."

"Well, I disagree," Lulu said, going to stand beside her brother. She wrapped an arm about his waist and grinned up at him. "I like having you here. I don't care what anyone in town has been saying!"

Tensing, Chase warned, "Lulu…"

"What?" The ebullient beekeeper turned around. "We're not going to talk about the elephant in the room? We have to! Sorry, Bridgett, but we have to discuss this."

Bridgett agreed. Cullen needed to know—directly from them—how much his family supported him.

Quietly, the nanny caught Jack's eye and ushered his children out to the back porch to play.

With the young audience gone, Lulu continued, "Personally, I think all the rumors were starting to force the price of your cattle down, even drive some potential buyers out entirely. Thank heaven Cartwright came along and saved the day with his bid. Talk about perfect timing!"

"It was, wasn't it," Cullen said. To Bridgett's dismay,

his cold, peremptory tone had everyone in the room staring and going silent. "The only question is," Cullen continued with sad resignation, "how did Dirk Cartwright happen to do just that?"

CULLEN WASN'T SURPRISED no one answered. Only his father seemed to know where he was going with this. Heart aching, he strode forward to confront the man whose respect he most wanted. The bitterness of all the years spent elsewhere clogged his throat. Reduced once again to the black sheep, illegitimate son, he rasped, "Tell me. How much did you have to pay Cartwright to offer me a job elsewhere?"

Rachel gasped, her hand flying to her throat.

Frank's gaze narrowed in steely warning. "Careful, son."

Cullen knew he should keep his feelings to himself, the way he had for years now. This once, however, he couldn't do it. Maybe because he had worked his ass off to earn his father's love and respect, only to have this brick wall between them remain.

Able to feel Bridgett quaking beside him, he kept his eyes locked with Frank's. Then he shook his head and shrugged off the soul-deep disappointment. "I understand why you'd want me gone. I'm nothing but a reminder of a time, with my mother, you to want to forget."

"You don't know what I want to remember and what I don't," Frank returned.

"Ah, maybe we should leave," Dan cut in uncomfortably.

"Nope," Frank said, his hard, uncompromising gaze still locked with Cullen's. "Everyone stay. We're having this out here and now."

Rachel, Lulu and Bridgett all eased onto the padded island stools. The men remained standing at various places along the counters.

Frank looked at Cullen, for once not about to mince words, either. "I loved my time with your mother. I would have married her, had she been willing. And I certainly would have stepped up from the get-go had I known she was carrying my child. But I didn't and we can't change that. All we can do is move forward with the love we should have had all along."

His eyes glistened as his voice grew hoarse. "And I do love you, Cullen. Every bit as much as I love my five other children and Rachel. You are a part of this family," he continued sternly. "You always will be. I know you've felt you never really belonged here, but you're wrong. You do."

Cullen stared at his dad, clearly taken aback by the emotional declaration.

"Would I go out of my way to help you succeed in business?" He shook his head. "That answer is more complicated."

Frank paused again. "If you came to me, asking for help, which you haven't, none of you have, I would consider it. But mostly," he continued, putting his arm around his wife, "I expect every single one of you to make your own way, the way Rachel and I did, and the way your mother apparently did, too, Cullen."

Cullen paused, accepting that.

Frank continued resolutely, "It is not the result that impresses me." He shrugged. "It never has been. It's the effort." He looked at all six of his children. "I want to know that whatever you decide to do, you've given it your best effort."

Silence fell.

Cullen continued to look at his father and Frank stared right back, a telltale glimmer in his gaze. Cullen felt his own eyes welling. Bridgett was tearing up, too. And they weren't the only ones.

Guilt spread through him, along with the relief.

Smiling, he realized, he wasn't being forced out.

No one here wanted him to go.

Especially and including the remarkable woman who had arranged the festivities.

"Now—" Frank scrubbed a hand over his face, a smile spreading "—last I heard, we had a celebration happening here…"

"I MADE A horse's ass out of myself, didn't I?" Cullen sighed, hours after everyone had finally left.

"Yes. But you and your dad hugged and made up, and everyone else was finally able to breathe a sigh of relief—because you both did say all that—and nothing happened except everyone finally knew what he and you were both thinking and feeling."

Fine lines appeared at the corners of his eyes, and he smiled. "It's funny. I never knew he loved me. He never said it. Until tonight."

Bridgett snuggled in the curve of his body, loving his warmth and his strength. "Maybe he didn't think he needed to. Maybe he thought you knew."

He slid his thumbs beneath her chin and raised her face to his. "You've got a point, darlin'," he told her tenderly. "None of us go around saying we love each other all the time, yet…we feel it…even when we're not physically together."

Bridgett turned her head slightly and kissed the center of Cullen's palm. "It's the same with my sibs."

They stood in the kitchen, locked in each other's arms, both baby and puppy contentedly sleeping in their beds.

Looking pretty relaxed and happy, too, Cullen exhaled and looked around. "It was a good party, wasn't it?"

"It was," Bridgett murmured.

The food had been a stellar impromptu Mexican feast. The hot sopaipillas, covered with confectioner's sugar and drizzled with homemade honey, had been the crowning glory.

Everyone had helped clean up, then gone home well fed and happy. The goodbye hugs had been long and fierce and genuine.

No one had commented further on the proposition Cullen had received. But Bridgett thought she knew what they all felt. Unable to stand the suspense any longer, she asked impulsively, "What are you going to do about the offer Dirk Cartwright made?" *Please don't tell me you're packing up and moving to Nebraska.*

Cullen exhaled, his expression maddeningly inscrutable. "Honestly? I don't know yet. I have to think about it."

It was what she had thought he would say, given the scope of the opportunity. Still, Bridgett could not deny she was disappointed.

He turned, backing her up against the counter. Caging her in with his arms on either side of her, he slanted his head over hers and lowered his mouth to hers. The kiss was an explosion of tenderness and heat, longing and fulfillment.

She knew he wasn't in love with her, but when they were together like this, she felt loved. Warm and safe. She felt secure in her life in a way she had never felt before.

They made their way to the bedroom and undressed each other in the moonlight. They kissed and stroked and caressed until she thought she would melt from the inside out. He reached into the nightstand and found a condom. She sheathed him, protecting them both.

Her eyes drifted shut as he parted her thighs and settled between them. Cupping her bottom, he lifted her toward him. Sliding home. Going deeper, and deeper still, until pleasure flooded her in fierce, unchecked waves. And then there was no more holding back. She shifted, so she was straddling his hips, her moan of ecstasy mingling with his.

And still he kissed her, taking her, the delicious glide in. And out. And back in…

He laid claim to her as no one ever had before. Kissing her breasts. Diving deep. Incoherent, she let her head fall back. Gave herself over to him and the feelings gathering deep inside her.

She'd thought she could separate love and desire. Make love with him without being *in love* with him.

She'd been wrong. He made her feel like a complete family was within her reach. That it was okay to want… everything. As long as it was with him. And, heaven help her, she did.

WEDNESDAY AFTERNOON, Mitzy summoned them to the Social Services office in San Angelo. The teenage girls were not being cooperative. It was Mitzy's hope Bridgett and Cullen might be able to help get the information they needed, so of course they agreed to go.

She and Cullen were silent on the drive, each of them wrapped in their own thoughts.

Finally, they walked into the building together. They signed in at the reception desk and made their way to the appropriate conference room, Bridgett carrying Robby and Cullen leading Riot.

Around the large table were the two teenagers, their parents, Dan and Mitzy. Sherri and Dawn both looked mutinous. And guilty.

"As you can see," Mitzy observed kindly, indicating

the baby and puppy with a tilt of her head, "Robby and Riot are both fine."

Dan added with law enforcement practicality, "But it's been a hard road for Bridgett, the nurse who found the baby and the puppy, and Cullen, the man who was charged with caring for them."

Actually, it hadn't been much of a burden at all.

It was not knowing what was going to happen next that was tearing her heart apart, Bridgett thought anxiously.

The girls couldn't take their eyes off the baby or the puppy.

They looked incredibly relieved, yet somehow awe-struck.

The way Mitzy was looking at her, silently beseeching her to take the lead, Bridgett knew it was up to her to somehow find a way to reach them and get them talking.

So, using the same approach she used with the parents of her tiny patients at the hospital N-ICU, she started with the truth.

"We're worried about Marie," Bridgett stated matter-of-factly, cuddling Robby close. "When a woman gives birth, she needs proper care during her pregnancy, the actual birth and the aftermath. If the mother doesn't get it at any one of those stages, there are a multitude of complications that can occur, some of them even life threatening. Plus, there are the emotional aspects of giving birth and surrendering a child to be dealt with."

She turned to Cullen.

He weighed in. "If you've helped her...we know you were too young to be thrust into this situation. That you stepped up, anyway, and did the best you could in a very difficult situation. And we want you to know we're all grateful." Cullen looked Sherri and Dawn in the eye. "Everyone last one of us."

Mitzy and Dan backed this up.

Bridgett pressed on emotionally. "But we still need to find Marie. Make sure she is okay."

"Can't she just go to a doctor anywhere?" Sherri asked belligerently.

"Why would she need to do it here—assuming she did have anything to do with this, anyway?" Dawn added hastily.

Firmly, Bridgett explained. "Because time is of the essence if Marie does have any kind of postpartum health problems."

Sherri bit her lip. "What would that look like?"

Bridgett listed the most obvious. "Fever. Flu-like symptoms. Soreness around the area of the birth canal. Menstrual-type bleeding that goes on and on…"

Sherri and Dawn both paled. Dawn said, "You're a nurse. Can't you help her?"

Bridgett was trying. "She really should be seen by an obstetrician."

Cullen cut in, "I think it might help Marie to physically see Robby and Riot, and know they are all right, too."

"Bottom line," Bridgett said, knowing it was the right thing to do, even as it cost her dearly. "Marie needs to know she still has options." Even as her heart was breaking, she paused to let the weight of her words sink in. "That nothing has been set in stone. She had no support system prior to this. We can and will give her that."

Whether through social services, or her—and perhaps Cullen's—own largesse, if need be.

"Then…" Bridgett took another deep breath, and pushed the words through the ache in her throat. "When Marie's had time to really think about it and consider, she can decide with an open heart and open mind what she wants to do. Give the baby and puppy over for adoption.

Or—" It was all she could do not to break into sobs herself as she prepared to give up what she wanted so dearly in order to do what her heart was telling her was the right and decent thing. "Or receive a lot of help—and there is a lot of that out there—and keep them."

Because, as much as Bridgett wanted to keep Robby and Riot, she was not going to do it at another woman's expense. Not under these horrific circumstances.

Sherri and Dawn looked at each other. "You'd really do that for her?" Dawn asked in amazement. Staring at her as if she were an angel just sent down from heaven.

Bridgett thought of Robby, who was so sweet, so innocent and untouched by all this. And Cullen, who'd suffered because he hadn't known his biological father for so long. And Marie, who apparently had grown up a burden to her own parents, feeling unwanted and unsupported. And probably unloved, as well.

Robby might not care now who had given birth to him. But one day he would. He'd want to know where he came from and why his birth mother had given him away. And though it would be difficult to face, in the long run it would be better for all involved if they used every avenue available to them to help his mother, the way they had helped him and his puppy companion. They all needed to know where—and with whom—Robby and Riot really and truly belonged.

Otherwise they'd always wonder. Always feel guilty. Always feel like maybe they hadn't done enough for everyone involved—and should have.

Bridgett looked at Mitzy, Dan and Cullen, the parents of the teens, the girls themselves.

They were staring at her as if they couldn't believe her unselfishness.

She knew she had surprised them. She had surprised

herself. She hadn't thought she had it in her to love and possibly let go.

She'd just found out she did.

Heaven help her, heaven help Cullen, she did.

Chapter Fifteen

An hour later, they finally had the news they had been waiting for. The two teens had confirmed what everyone else had long suspected, that Cullen was not related to Robby biologically in any way. And Marie Griffin had been found at Dawn's family's vacation home on Lake Laramie.

Cullen and Bridgett left the family crisis center and made their way to the Laramie Community Hospital, where the teenage mother had been taken. Mitzy Martin arrived just ahead of them and was there to greet them. Bridgett had called Violet and Gavin, and they'd taken Robby and Riot to their home nearby.

"How is she?" Bridgett asked, her nurse's training kicking in.

Mitzy had just spoken with the ER doctor. "Dehydrated. Suffering from a mild pelvic infection. A few days in the hospital with some IV fluids and antibiotics and she should be okay."

Bridgett and Cullen breathed a mutual sigh of relief.

In full social-worker mode, Mitzy escorted them to the second floor. "I filled Marie in about the two of you taking care of Robby and Riot. She asked to speak to you both. So if you-all are okay with that…?"

Bridgett looked at Cullen, unsure where the latest developments left the two of them, since his name had now been cleared. "Do you want to do this together?"

"Wouldn't have it any other way," he said gruffly.

He took her hand and gave it a hard, reassuring squeeze. Their gazes meshed and they took a simultaneous breath, then walked in.

Marie Griffin was sitting up in a hospital bed, an IV in her arm. Her long, curly brown hair was drawn into a low ponytail. Clad in a hospital gown, covers pulled up to her waist, she looked pale and anxious. And so very young and vulnerable.

Mitzy Martin made introductions then eased away from the bed so Cullen and Bridgett could step in.

Marie swallowed. "I guess you remember me?"

Cullen nodded. "You and your friends were at the high school Career Fair in San Angelo last fall."

Marie flashed a wan, grateful smile. "You came to talk to us about ranching and what it meant to you. How you moved around a lot when you were a kid, but even when you felt your dog, Riot, was your only friend, you were always able to find something worthwhile and satisfying to do on the ranch."

"You asked a lot of questions."

Marie sighed wistfully. "I always wanted to live on a ranch. Work with horses. Maybe cattle, too. I just couldn't figure out a way to make it happen." She knitted her hands together.

Bridgett saw her nails were bitten to the quick.

"But I knew I was going to have to do something since all the rest of my dreams had just gone bust." In a halting voice, she told them about the clandestine romance she'd had with a boy she'd met at a weekend-long concert in Houston the previous summer. By the time she realized he had been lying to her about everything, including his name and phone number, he had disappeared and she was pregnant. Unable to turn to her parents, she'd gone to a couple of her girlfriends for help.

"I had a lot of time to think about who I wanted to give my kid to when he or she was born, and I kept going back to Cullen. He seemed so good and kind. And he sort of looked like the baby daddy, too." She released a quavering breath. "And then, when Riot showed up on my doorstep, just a tiny shivering little thing last February, I thought of the stray dog that Cullen found when he was a kid. It seemed like a huge sign. So my girlfriends and I figured out a plan to take them both to the Laramie fire station and leave them for Cullen."

"Except I found them," Bridgett put in.

"I know. We saw. We were hiding a short distance away, just to make sure that Robby and Riot got found. When they did, we went back to the lake house."

"Where you've been ever since," Cullen said gently.

Tears shining in her eyes, Marie nodded.

Bridgett took her hand. "You don't have to run anymore. Cullen and I will be here to see that you and Robby and Riot get everything you need."

"You mean that?" Marie's lower lip trembled.

Bridgett looked at Cullen. He nodded in solidarity. "We do."

"I just have one question."

They waited.

Marie's chin quivered. She regarded Bridgett soberly. "Mitzy told me that you've been fostering them. I know you've been taking great care of both Robby and Riot, on Cullen's ranch, and that Cullen has been helping out a lot, too. But…do you think you could ever love them? The way I can't? The way really great parents always do?"

Bridgett nodded, her heart bursting wide open. "Oh,

honey, I already do." She bit her lip, trying hard not to cry. "I have since the start."

Marie turned. "What about you, Cullen?"

His eyes filled with emotion. He closed his fist and tapped the region over his heart in the age-old sign of love and solidarity. "They're right here, kid," he finally said in a rusty-sounding voice. "They always will be." He paused. "No matter what happens."

He was doing the decent thing, just as Bridgett had. Giving the troubled teen an emotional out from a decision she'd made under extreme duress. Bridgett appreciated his valor. Knew it was the right thing to do, even as she mourned their own potential loss. But wasn't that what being a parent was all about? Caring for your children, then letting them go, when life demanded it?

Marie paused, looking uncertain and conflicted again. "I don't know if I still have any rights, but…would all of you…" She burst into tears, then turned to Mitzy, too. "Would it be okay for me to see them again?" She dabbed at her eyes. "Because I feel like I really need to be with them, at least one more time."

A PART OF Bridgett had always known it was possible that whoever had left Robby and Riot in such distress would have a change of heart. Resurface. Ask for a second chance.

Experiencing it, however, was more numbing and heartrending than even she'd expected.

Cullen seemed awfully quiet, too, as they picked up Robby and Riot and drove back to the ranch.

"Are you okay?" Cullen asked finally, as they neared the Western Cross. His large hands gripped the steering wheel. "Because you don't have to be the one to take Riot and Robby to the hospital to visit Marie tomorrow. Mitzy and I can do it."

Why put off the inevitable? Especially if this was where fate was leading them.

"No." Bridgett girded her heart. "I think it's important Marie see them—now that she's in a place she can get the help she would need to keep them." Help that a few weeks ago the runaway teen didn't think was even possible. She swallowed. "I don't want to bail—just because things might not go my way. I owe it to everyone to see this through." That was what being a foster mother was about. Loving, and then doing what was right for everyone in the end, even if it was agonizing for her.

She slanted Cullen a glance. He seemed to fill the cab.

"I feel that way, too," he admitted, reaching over to take her hand in a grip that was as strong and reassuring as ever.

Bridgett drew from his courage. "In any case, we have at least one more night with them. I'd really like to savor it."

And they did. Having what could very well be their last "family" dinner out on the back porch. Taking both puppy and baby for a long walk around the Western Cross. Lingering over the nightly bedtime routine.

Meeting up in the master bedroom, when Riot and Robby were both sound asleep, to make love one last, bittersweet time. At least, that was the way she saw it. Cullen, however, had other ideas.

"This is our destiny, Bridgett," he told her, holding her close.

The irony of the situation was not lost on her. Nor should it be on him. She flushed as her emotions rose. "Let's not romanticize this, Cullen. If this path to family closes, another one will open up."

"I'll make sure it does," he promised, his expression suddenly one of concern. "But sometimes in life you have to let things play out the way they're meant to." Even though waiting was the hardest part.

They made love throughout the night, and the next day took both puppy and baby to the hospital. The visit was a pleasant one. As they convened in the rooftop solarium, Marie asked a ton of questions about both Robby and Riot. She petted the puppy and held the baby briefly, then turned both back over to Bridgett and Cullen, watching the way they interacted with each other.

In between subsequent visits over the next couple of days, she met privately with Mitzy, and a psychologist and counselor.

Finally, Marie was well enough to be released.

And she made her decision.

Mitzy made the trip out to the Western Cross to tell Bridgett and Cullen the news. "Marie wants the two of you to adopt Robby and keep Riot."

Bridgett did a double take. Relieved and yet... "Together?"

"Marie has thought about it and thinks two loving parents would be way better than just one."

Obviously drawing on his own childhood difficulties, Cullen said gruffly, "Can't disagree with her there."

Although Bridgett knew that was true, the last thing she wanted to do was back Cullen into a corner, the way her ex had once tried to force her into something she'd wanted in the long run but wasn't ready for at that moment.

Determined to give him an out, the same way she had given Marie one, she pointed out quietly, "But we're not married."

Mitzy shot back, "Are you going to be?"

Put on the spot, Bridgett flushed and shrugged. She couldn't quite look Cullen in the eye. "I don't even know how to answer that," she mumbled finally.

Neither, apparently, did Cullen, judging by his silence.

Mitzy continued, "Because it would make a difference with the court, if you are. In any case, Marie is prepared to surrender all rights to the baby and the puppy as long as one or both of you follow through on your promise to care for the child. So we can put your wish to become mutually responsible in the same petition or separate ones. Or go back to the original plan and just let Bridgett foster-adopt on her own."

"And in the meantime?" Cullen asked.

"Formally," Mitzy explained, "Robby and Riot remain with Bridgett, since she is the approved foster mother."

Bridgett cleared her throat. All along she had been prepared for everything but this—figuring out what exactly she and Cullen meant to each other.

Was it real?

Or was it an infatuation—at least on his part—generated by the way they had been playing house? "Do I have leeway about where I care for them while I figure everything out?" Bridgett asked.

"Yes." Mitzy smiled. "You can stay at the Western Cross, if that works for all of you. Or move in with family. In the department's eyes, you've more than proven yourself a stellar foster parent, Bridgett, so really, it's up to you."

Except it wasn't.

Because if she wanted to stay, she would be putting Cullen on the spot.

His own emotions under wraps, Cullen asked, "What about the foster-adoption? If I ask to be included in that, is the court going to approve my request?"

"If you were married to Bridgett? Both petitioning to formally adopt? Yes, it would be a sure thing. Especially, Cullen, since you are one of the McCabes and Bridgett is a Monroe, to whom family is all."

"Except…" Bridgett hated to point it out, yet again. "Cullen and I aren't married." They weren't technically even dating!

A heavy silence fell between them as the implications of all that was at stake hung in the air.

Finally, Cullen asked, "What happens in regard to the baby's biological father?"

Mitzy frowned. "There were ten thousand people at that music festival in Houston. Even if she had a picture of the father—which she apparently does not—she doesn't have his real name or phone number. There's no way to track him down."

So Robby would never know the identity of his biological father, Bridgett realized, as Cullen hadn't for so many years.

"What will the birth certificate say?" Cullen asked.

"That the father is unknown. Until he is formally adopted," Mitzy admitted. "Then, if Robby has an adoptive father, the birth certificate can be legally changed to reflect that."

Reason enough, Bridgett thought, knowing Cullen's gallant, loving and caring heart, for him to go forward. And while that might be—probably was—the right thing to do for Robby, was it the right thing to do for the two of them? Especially if their relationship was based on friendship and passion rather than love? It was one thing to carry on an affair, with no real ties holding them down or back. Another, to find themselves boxed in by circumstances beyond their control.

Her breath hitched. They'd been so focused on solving the mystery, clearing Cullen's name and caring for Robby and Riot, she and Cullen hadn't given any thought to their relationship in the long term. All he had said, when pressed, was that he wanted to concentrate on the "here and now."

Not wanting to find out that it was mutual loneliness plus crisis propelling them together, she swallowed, focusing on things that were easier for her to deal with emotionally. "What about Marie? What is going to happen to her?"

Mitzy sighed sadly. "She was right about her parents. We finally tracked them down. And they want nothing to do with Marie or her problems. So she is going to a girls' ranch in North Texas for the next two years. She's very excited about it. She's going to be able to work with horses, finish high school and get the counseling and group therapy she needs to recover from her ordeal, as well as start community college. They'll help her get loans and scholarships."

"Will she stay in touch?"

"She's open to it, eventually, if you are. Right now, though, she wants to concentrate on getting her life together." Mitzy gathered up her things. "Look, I know you need to think about all of this. Talk it over. Obviously it is a big decision, so I want you to take your time."

Cullen turned to Bridgett as Mitzy drove down the lane. He seemed as relieved as she was fraught with anxiety. "Congratulations, Mom."

Not sure whether she should say "Congratulations Dad!" or not, Bridgett held up a staying hand. Her feelings an incredible jumbled-up mess, she countered in a low, strangled voice, "Let's not go there just yet."

He released an impatient breath. "Why not?"

"I don't want to jinx it. There are still so many things that could go wrong."

"Not if we get married. Then it sounds like it will be a slam dunk."

Bridgett's mouth opened in an O of surprise. "What did you say?"

"You heard Mitzy. Getting approved won't be a problem if we get married."

"For the baby?"

"And the puppy. And us," he retorted cheerfully. "We make a great team, Bridgett. The last few weeks have shown us that."

Her overwhelming need for him to be happy remained intact. He would not be, if he never experienced the kind of all-encompassing love she still wanted. Not that their relationship would immediately crash and burn. They'd probably be fine for a while. But then one of two things would happen. He'd either realize he had settled, in marrying her, or he'd fall in love with someone else and be torn between what he had already promised and what he wanted and needed. Either way, they'd be miserable and brokenhearted. Robby and Riot would suffer, too. The way he had suffered when his mother had split up with Buck.

Resolved to limit the damage as much as she could, she reminded him of all the success that still lay ahead for him. "You have an offer to buy a huge ranch in Nebraska."

He stared at her, looking every bit as blindsided as she felt when he had offered to marry her in order to give Robby a daddy and make the foster-adoption go smoother.

"So?" The happiness left his eyes. In its place, something hard and forbidding took over.

Her throat ached almost as much as her heart. "So, if we were to get married you would have to stay here, with us."

He stepped back and ran his hands through his hair.

"I thought that was what you'd want," he snapped, looking confused.

Her eyes burning, she replied warily. "Not if it makes you feel trapped. I was nearly forced into marriage with Aaron because he wanted to have kids right away. It was a miserable experience. Having lived it, I can't put anyone else through it."

He stared at her in mounting disappointment. "So you're saying that clinching the adoption is the *only* reason you'd marry me."

Hurt he would think she was saying this because she had no regard for his feelings, she stepped forward and countered, as calmly as possible, "I'm saying it's not enough reason to rush into anything. I can petition to adopt right away without slowing things down. You can petition, too, if you decide not to go to Nebraska, and go through the home study and the background checks and all of that."

"And if I don't go. Would you and Robby and Riot stay here with me or live elsewhere?"

Talk about a loaded question!

She shrugged, feeling every bit as boxed in as he. Like they needed to take a step back. Give each other a little time to breathe. Think about what they each really felt. "I'd move in with Bess." Hopefully, temporarily. "The point is, if you do decide to stay and foster-adopt with me, we could still see each other all the time—without actually living together."

His face was a bland, polite mask. "You don't have any doubts about taking on Robby and Riot?"

"No, of course not." Where was he going with this?

He folded his arms in front of him, all too ready to judge her. Unfairly. "But you do have doubts about hitching your wagon to mine."

"No, but I'm saying this has all happened awfully fast for you, Cullen. I've been on the foster-adopt list for the last two years. For you, even the idea of parenthood and sharing your life with anyone is all brand-new. When the novelty wears off and reality hits, and you have to decide whether to keep flipping ranches and expanding your horizons or staying here, waiting for the right land to open up, you may not be so happy."

He looked at her, incredulous. "So it's all on me."

Defiantly, she held her ground. "Why are you twisting everything I say?"

He caught her by the shoulders. "Because I think my issues have nothing to do with your reluctance to marry me." Hurt and resentment underscored his low tone.

Blinking back tears, she splayed her hands across his chest, holding him at bay. "Then what does?"

He stared at her as if she was a stranger. "Your notions of destiny. Of finding a romance so big it will never fade."

She inhaled sharply, not about to mislead him. "I admit I want what three of my siblings have and my parents had," she said stiffly. "What my twin and I still lack. A relationship that is so strong and so right it will last a lifetime."

He gave her a slow, critical once-over. "And you don't think we have that."

I might if you'd ever once said you loved me, she thought miserably. Or could love me. Or were falling in love with me.

But you haven't. So...

She wrested herself from his arms as hot, stinging tears raced down her face. "I know you desire me, Cullen." She swallowed around the increasing ache in her throat. "I know we work well together and we can have fun together, and we even want the same things for Riot and Robby, but...*is that enough*?" Could it ever be?

Anger flared in his navy blue eyes. "Obviously not for you." He spun away from her.

"Where are you going?" she cried, aware this could easily blow up into something neither of them wanted.

Grimacing, he tossed the words over his shoulder. "Out. To clear my head."

Her pulse took on a rapid staccato beat as the loving home they'd built over the last two weeks quickly devolved into the last place she would ever want to be. A place that was attractive and orderly on the surface, but chaotic and numbing underneath. Swiftly, she closed the distance between them. "You're leaving us?"

"No," he said, in the same take-no-prisoners voice he had used on her that first day in the hospital corridor, when he thought she'd been playing a very bad joke on him. "I made a commitment to Robby and to Riot, to keep them in my heart and always take care of them," he said softly but firmly. "I'm not reneging on that."

Her heart broke. "Just me."

For a long moment, she thought he was going to say something, but he didn't. He merely drew an equalizing breath. "We'll find a way to coparent. To have a friendly, cordial relationship. But given the way you feel about me and what we've had..." He paused and shook his head in silent remonstration, a look that went deeper than any hurt she had ever sustained. "It's clear to me now that the two of us building upon anything more than that is just not going to be possible." And on that note, he walked out, shutting the door behind him.

Shattering her heart in the process.

Chapter Sixteen

"I've been showing you houses all afternoon that would be fantastic for you and your family, and you haven't liked any of them," Jeanne Phipps complained, several days later.

Bess grinned. "I'm beginning to think she doesn't really want to leave that ranch she is living on."

Bridgett pushed Robby in his stroller around the landscaped backyard. Past the outdoor playset with the toddler-size slide, and the baby swing that would be just perfect in a few months.

"Don't start, you two."

She didn't know why she couldn't imagine living here, even with her twin as her housemate—but she just couldn't. "We'll find the place. Eventually." Although nothing she had seen thus far had even come close to the home she was still living in—albeit in a slightly estranged way—with Cullen.

Jeanne assessed Bridgett's inner tumult with a glance. "How about I let the two of you talk before we see any other properties on the list? I have a few calls to make, anyway." She strode off, her high heels clicking on the pavers.

The back gate snapped shut.

Bess sat down on one of the wicker chairs on the patio.

The leashed Riot dropped down beside her. "Why don't you just admit what's going on with you?"

Too restless to sit down, Bridgett kept rolling the contentedly sleeping Robby back and forth. "And what would that be?"

"You regret turning down Cullen's marriage proposal."

Regret didn't begin to cover it. Not a second went by without her wishing she could have followed her heart and said yes. Instead of listening to her head.

Miserably, she countered, "He doesn't love me, Bess. Not in the all-encompassing way you need to love someone you marry and intend to spend a lifetime with."

"Could have fooled me. And everyone else who has seen the two of you together.'"

"Me, too, for a while, anyway." Until there at the end he'd shown what he was really thinking and feeling. Or *not* feeling.

"Cullen is a man of his word, Bess. When this whole thing started, we made a deal. I would do everything I could to help him preserve his good name and not bring shame on the McCabe family."

"By letting him help you with Robby and Riot, even though they weren't his."

"Right. And, in turn, he promised to do everything within his power to help me get approved to foster-adopt Robby and Riot. Suggesting we marry was just a way to expedite that process and ensure the outcome."

Bess scoffed. "It had nothing to do with how much he has come to care for you and Robby and Riot?"

"We're friends."

Bess lifted a brow.

"And lovers."

Another pause.

"And we have successfully coparented."

Bess petted Riot. "So, what else do you need to be happy?"

Bridgett sighed. "In the long run? A lot more."

"You don't think it's destiny?"

That was the hell of it; the emotional side of her still did. The intellectual side of her did not.

Bridgett drew a deep breath. "The crisis brought us together, Bess. Not knowing what was going to happen with Robby and Riot, or where they came from. Struggling to care for them together intensified all that." *Gave us a false sense of intimacy that I sentimentally interpreted as way more than that.* "And now..." She swallowed, unable to continue.

"Now what?" Bess pressed.

Bridgett stiffened her spine. "He was very clear when this whole situation arose that the only reason he was participating was out of honor and responsibility." He hadn't seen the situation as their destiny. Or been looking to get married. Or have kids—the way she had for some time now.

"So?" Bess squinted over at her. "That's admirable in a way that only adds to his allure. Not every guy I know would have stepped up the way he did."

Anguished tears stung Bridgett's eyes. "Don't you think I know that?" He'd kindly offered them his home and his help, and to a certain extent, anyway, his heart...

"Then what's the problem?" her sister persisted.

Knotting her hands together, Bridgett struggled to explain, "Cullen is a McCabe. He still wants to do the right thing. And the right thing in his mind, the easy thing that would make everyone happy—at least in the short term— is for him to marry me. And for us to live together like a real family."

Bess arched a brow in Bridgett's direction. "Like the real family you've been the last few weeks?"

It had been a fairy tale. But fairy tales did not last. Any more than relationships forged in crises did. She couldn't bear to see their happiness deteriorate bit by bit as cold reality returned. "I can't take advantage of his generosity." And that's what she would be doing. So she had to be as noble now, as he had been.

"I see." Bess regarded her gravely. "So you'll break his heart, instead."

Bridgett flushed.

Silence fell.

Bess stood to square off with her. "Have you told him how you feel?"

"Yes."

Bess grasped her forearms. "I mean really, sis. Deep down."

Bridgett jerked her arms free. Unable to bear the scrutiny, she walked away. "I told you. I don't want to back him into a corner." The way her ex had once tried to pressure her into doing something she wasn't convinced she wanted, never mind was actually ready for…

"So what's the alternative?" Bess threw up her hands in frustration. "Live a lie?"

Stubbornly, Bridgett tried to hold on to what she could. "It's not like Cullen and I are giving up everything," she argued.

"Isn't it?"

Bridgett moved the stroller closer, spoke softly so as not to disturb the sleeping infant. "We're on the verge of being friends now. Coparents, if the court and Department of Children and Family Services agree." Or, at least, they were trying to accomplish all that. Since their falling out, their interactions were excruciatingly polite. Stilted. And while she hoped the awkwardness would ease, over time, she could not guarantee it.

Bess looked as disappointed as Bridgett felt. "Are you telling me you'd be happy with that?"

"No, but…" Bridgett shrugged and dug in all the harder. "I was prepared to be happy with a whole lot less when I signed up to foster-adopt as a single mom."

Her twin looked at her long and hard. "Maybe," Bess said softly, "that's always been the problem."

"A LITTLE LONELY around here?"

Cullen turned to see his stepmother, Rachel, striding toward him. He turned away from the fence post he had been repairing. "Always is when I auction off a big part of my herd." That would change in a few weeks, when the new crop of Hotlander calves were born. Then life would be busy again. Almost as busy as it had been when he and Bridgett and the baby and Riot were a team.

Though not as happy…

Not anywhere near as happy…

"That's not what I'm talking about." Rachel strode closer, scolding. "And you know it, Cullen McCabe!"

Obviously, she'd heard that Bridgett was off looking at houses again. Not that he hoped she would find anything. Because until she did, she and the baby and the puppy would be staying right there on the ranch with him. And though they weren't exactly getting along famously—at least, not in the intimate way they once had—it was still good to have them nearby. Comforting, almost. If you could overlook their almost unbearably fake cordiality, anyway.

"You forgot the Reid." He pointed out the omission of his middle name in an effort to change the subject.

"Yes, I did!" Rachel shot back fiercely, surprising

him. "Although I wouldn't have—if I thought you were as proud of being a Reid as you are of being a McCabe." She strode even closer, her boots digging into the manicured grass. The empathy he'd come to expect from her lit her eyes. "It made sense when you first came to live with us. You'd always been a Reid and then, suddenly, with the truth about your paternity discovered, you were a McCabe, too."

That had been a rocky time.

Rachel studied him with a lawyer's assessing gaze. "But now the use of both surnames just seems to drag you down. Make you feel fifty percent McCabe, fifty percent Reid, instead of one hundred percent McCabe and one hundred percent Reid."

Hadn't she just hit the nail on the head, he ruminated sagely. Cullen shrugged, embarrassed to find his mother's selfishness and his illegitimacy could still embarrass him. "I think it's understandable why I don't quite fit in anywhere," he muttered. At least, he hadn't. Until Bridgett and Robby and Riot came along and made a home with him. Then, for a short while, at the Western Cross, he had.

He went back to stringing barbed wire. "Not the way the rest of my half siblings do."

Rachel stood next to the section he was repairing. She folded her arms in front of her. "Do you think your feelings about yourself would have been different if Frank had known you as his son from the beginning? That your life would have been better, somehow?"

An honest question deserved an honest answer. "For me? Probably. I don't know how it would have been for you and him, given the fact that the two of you were newlyweds and my mom not really the sharing type."

Rachel nodded in understanding. "In any case, we can't change what was."

"I know that."

Her expression softening, she reached out to touch his arm. "Then why do you keep punishing yourself?"

He ignored the brief, familial touch. "I'm not."

"You let Bridgett and Robby and Riot go without a fight," she pointed out gently, stepping back.

They hadn't actually left yet. But they would, as soon as Bridgett found a place, and then life as they knew it really would be over. Cullen met his stepmother's steady glance, squared his shoulders. "It was what Bridgett wanted."

Rachel seemed skeptical. "Sure about that?"

Unfortunately, he was. "I suggested we get married," Cullen stated tersely. "And instead of saying yes, as I had hoped, she said there was no reason to rush into anything."

"She could have a point, given how fast everything has happened."

If it were only that, Cullen would have agreed. Figuring he had done enough for one day, he began packing up his tools. "She also wants to continue on with a solo adoption rather than refile completely so I can join her."

Rachel's brows lifted at his terse tone. "She's opposed to you becoming Robby's legal father?"

He strode back over to his pickup. "No. She just wants it to happen separately from her petition to foster-adopt."

Rachel followed. "Because she doesn't trust you to be around?"

Because she wants some big wildly romantic love that he had failed to give her.

And if she couldn't have that, she would prefer to go on romantically unattached. As a single mother. As friends. And nothing more.

"Something like that," he fibbed.

Rachel watched him pull off his work gloves. "Is that

the way you feel? Like you want to move on? Maybe take that tremendous opportunity in Nebraska?"

Even though it felt like he was being pushed away with both hands, leaving was the last thing on his mind. And that was weird, Cullen acknowledged silently. Usually, in a situation like this, he would have already been packed and on his way to his next ranch to flip. Or, in this case, to the Cartwright Ranch in Nebraska to take advantage of what was still a very big opportunity.

Something about the way his stepmom was looking at him, however, tempted him to respond more candidly than usual.

He dropped the toolbox into the bed of his truck. Tossed the excess barbed wire in after that. "The truth?"

Rachel flashed an encouraging grin. "Nothing but."

Taking her up on her offer of a shoulder to lean on, he confessed, "The whole thing has left me feeling blind-sided."

She nodded, to her credit, not at all surprised. "Completely understandable."

He exhaled wearily. "And I'm lonely as hell." He bit down on a curse as soon as the words were out of his mouth. Had he actually said that aloud? He guessed he had.

Rachel rocked back on the heels of her cowgirl boots, looking more ranch wife, now, than attorney. "I figured as much." She stopped to search his face. "But that's the way you've always been, isn't it?"

He didn't answer. Didn't have to. This woman who had breezed into his life without a prayer of taking his deceased mother's place knew his heart like nobody else. Always had, always would. Rachel edged closer. To his shock, tears suddenly blurred her eyes. "I blame myself for that, you know," she said thickly.

He stared. "Why?" He reached inside his truck and retrieved a box of tissues, handed them over. "You welcomed me with open arms when not many women in your place would have."

Rachel took several and blotted her eyes. "I also did you a terrible disservice." She shook her head in obvious regret. "When you first came to us, with that impenetrable shield of politeness, this obvious determination not to be a bother to anyone, your dad wanted to tear it down. *Force* you to tackle the difficulties and become a McCabe from the get-go."

Sounded like Frank.

It was also the way he would have treated any of his five other kids.

Rachel blew her nose. "But I wouldn't let him," she confessed, distraught. "I told him how overwhelmed I had been when I first married into the iconic Texas McCabe clan. How I had only become family bit by bit, and because of all you had been through, he needed to give you the *room* to absorb it all, on your own terms, in your own time."

The overwhelming emotion in her low voice had his own throat tightening. "You were right," he told her hoarsely, knowing how fragile he had been, how afraid he'd been of losing what he had left of the only life he had ever known—and his late mother.

But, on the other hand, if Frank had done that—treated him just like his siblings, instead of with kid gloves, maybe there wouldn't have been such a feeling of apartness all these years.

Rachel touched his forearm gently. "Actually," she corrected, practical and empathetic as ever, "your dad and I both were right in our approach. He should have pushed you more, made you see that he did care deeply about you, had from the very first moment he found out about you. In fact, in some ways, I think he and I both loved you more than your siblings at that stage because we hadn't been given the chance to know you earlier. So we were making up for lost time." She teared up again. "I just wish you had seen that."

He wrapped his arms around her, pulling her in like the family he had always wanted her to be. "I knew it, Rachel. I felt it." Deep in his soul and his heart.

She hugged him back with maternal ferocity. Then shifted back far enough to allege sadly, pragmatically, "You just didn't return the emotions."

Feeling the moment turn awkward again, Cullen dropped his arms. "I did." He studied her wary expression. "I just…didn't trust it. For my mom, love—romantic love, family love, love of friends—it all always faded." The way Bridgett's had apparently diminished for him.

Rachel shook her head. "From what I know, you are probably right about your mother's love for everyone else, but not about what she felt for you, Cullen. I'm betting that was incredibly fierce from beginning to end. Otherwise, she wouldn't have taken such pains to have you with her all those years. She wouldn't have been afraid to share you with the rest of your kin."

Rachel paused to let him absorb what she was saying.

When she was certain it had registered, she took both his hands tightly in hers. "If your mother hadn't loved you with all her heart, Cullen, she could have left you with your dad at any time. She knew that. But she didn't. Instead, she made the best life she could for you."

She had, at that.

"Yes, it was a mistake, keeping you and your dad apart, but you have each other now." Rachel sniffed again and continued in a low, quavering voice. "And that counts for a heck of a lot, doesn't it?"

"It does." Knowing this had to be said, and said now, Cullen pushed the rusty-sounding words out. "And Rachel? Just for the record? As long as we're being clear here?" He looked her in the eye. "You mean an awful lot to me, too."

Her eyes shone.

They were silent.

She embraced him fiercely. "I want you to be happy and fulfilled, Cullen. And the only way that is ever going to happen," she warned, "is if you stop holding back and seize the opportunity in front of you. Talk to your dad, Cullen. Start letting him be there for you the way he has always wanted to be. And after that? Open up your heart to Bridgett, too."

They talked a little more, then Rachel left. Buoyed by her pep talk, Cullen returned to the ranch house, and began to prepare for what he was determined would be the most important evening of his life thus far.

He had just finished seasoning a couple of porterhouse steaks, when he got the text from Bridgett. Headed back to the ranch. Finally know what our next steps should be.

Our next steps.

He wasn't sure what that meant, given that she intended to leave the Western Cross as soon as possible. Had she found a place? Decided to take Lucille Lockhart up on her offer, after all, and made a move-out plan she wanted to share with him? Or was she simply speaking in temporary generalities?

Hoping it was the latter, he poured premade salad into a bowl, put a couple of Idaho potatoes into the oven to bake and made sure there was charcoal in the grill. He had wine, too. Although he wasn't sure she would want any.

Finished, he stepped out onto the front porch to wait for the little group he'd come to think of as his family. It wasn't long before he saw Bridgett's SUV coming up the drive. He walked out to help her, but only she emerged from the vehicle. He shoved aside his fear that this really was the end for them, and forced a welcoming smile. "Where are Robby and Riot?"

"In town, with my family. I told them I'd pick them up later, after we'd talked."

Looked like he had one last chance to make things right. He damn well was not going to squander it. He escorted her away from the SUV. "Before you begin, I have some things to say to you, too."

Suddenly, she looked as apprehensive as he felt. "Okay," she said softly, setting down her bag and taking a place on the front steps of the ranch house. "I'm listening."

He settled next to her. "The last few days have given me a lot of time to think." She turned to him, her gaze intent, giving him courage. "I've realized some things about myself." He forced himself to go on with unflinching honesty. "My flipping ranches was more than just a way to amass the cash I needed to build a cattle-breeding business for myself. It was also a way to continually cut ties and keep from putting down roots. Just the way my mom did when I was growing up."

It hadn't brought them happiness, in either case.

Bridgett studied him with keen understanding. "And yet you succumbed to family pressure and came back to Laramie, anyway," she pointed out softly, covering his hand with her own.

"I wanted to belong here," he admitted, weaving his fingers through the slender grip of hers. "I just didn't know how to make things better with my dad and the rest of the family. But you're right." He grimaced at the rusty sound of his voice. "Deep down, I hoped buying a ranch and setting up a cow-calf operation here would earn me the approval I craved from Frank and Rachel and the others."

He exhaled.

"Unfortunately, the Western Cross was no more a real home to me than any of the other places I have lived." With a rueful grin, he admitted, "Until you and Robby and Riot moved in. Then it became the place I'd always wanted and dreamed of having." *The place where we all belonged.*

"I thought it was perfect, too, not just for you, but for all of us," Bridgett confided softly, meeting his eyes. "At least—" her lower lip took on a disappointed slant "—until you got that big offer to sell out and move to Nebraska."

"About that." He tightened his grip on her hand. "I formally turned it down the day we found Marie Griffin. I just didn't have a chance to tell you. And then, with everything going on…I wasn't sure it mattered. But it does now," he told her firmly. "I want to put down roots in Laramie County. I want to be here with you and Robby and Riot."

She wanted to believe him; he could see that.

"What about your dream of owning as many acres as your dad does?" she asked in a low, quavering voice.

"That can still happen right here in Texas. If I'm patient, and I promise you I will be."

Her slender shoulders relaxed.

She looked over at him, her cheeks flushing self-consciously. "Now, on to why *I* wanted to talk to *you* about next steps."

He tensed, his heart thudding in his chest. This could be bad or this could be good.

"You aren't the only one who has done a lot of soul-searching. First, I've redefined what home is to me. When I met you, I thought all I needed was to buy that perfect little bungalow I had my eye on." Still holding his gaze, she bit her lip and plunged on. "But I've realized home isn't comprised of the right-sized walls and a sturdy roof over your head. Or even the much valued fenced-in back yard with playset that I was convinced I would need to please DCFS. It's a place where you feel safe and warm and loved. And that," she said, her voice breaking slightly, "can be anywhere we hang our hats."

We…

Did she mean all four of them?

Or was she speaking metaphorically?

Her expression was so serious and intent, he had no clue.

She took another deep breath. Plunged on. "Second, I think the real reason I've been so hung up on destiny all this time is because I haven't wanted to be responsible for my own happiness." She shook her head in heartfelt regret. "I wanted bliss to magically fall into my lap, like a twist of fate, and until it did—" she took another shuddering breath "—I had made up my mind not to pursue anything but safe bets."

She reached over and squeezed his hand. "I didn't want to be involved with anything that had even the tiniest potential to hurt me. It's why I felt I couldn't foster a child unless it was available to adopt."

He could understand that, now that he had faced the possibility of loving a family he considered his only to lose them.

Her hand tightened on his. "I knew chances were slim to none of that happening, given the long waiting lists and the fact I was single and had no experience fostering, but

I thought if I waited long enough, that would magically happen, anyway."

He tucked an errant lock of hair behind her ear. "Except for one thing, Bridgett. You did find Robby and Riot. And the note left with them led you to me." *And all of that to us.*

"That was definitely a life-changing miracle."

He nodded in agreement.

Her soul laid bare, she continued confiding. "But again, I didn't know as much about myself as I thought I did. Because the experience with Marie taught me I could be more selfless than I ever imagined." For a silent moment she searched his eyes. "It helped me realize that love comes in all sorts of ways. You just have to be open to it. And that's what I want, Cullen."

She stood, drawing him to his feet, too, and splayed her arms across his chest. "I want this ranch that has come to make us all feel so safe and loved and cared for, be home to all of us." Her lower lip trembled and tears filled her eyes. "I want love—with you. Family love. Passionate love. The love that comes between two friends. And two parents. And two people." Her voice quavered with all the affection he had ever wanted to receive. "Two people who one day just might not be able to live without each other."

The tentative, hopeful note in her voice filled him with joy unlike anything he had ever felt. "I think we've already reached that point," he admitted gruffly, pulling her all the way into his arms and holding her close. "That's what I was waiting here to tell you. I finally know where I belong and with whom." No longer afraid, he took the final leap and laid bare his heart and soul, too. "I love you, Bridgett, with every fiber of my being. And I'm never, ever going to stop."

She flung her arms about his neck. Tears glittered on

her eyelashes and spilled down her face. "Oh, Cullen, I love you, too. So much."

Her heartfelt confession filled him with warmth and tenderness. He paused to kiss her, again and again, her face cupped in his hands. As long as they were spilling all, he had to be completely honest with her. "I know you said you didn't want to get married." *At least, not right now.*

She silenced him with an index finger against his lips. "I fibbed. I do. Very much."

"I do, too." The peace he'd wanted stealing through his heart, he warned, "But I want to do it when we both agree we are ready and the time is right."

She grinned. "Right back at you, cowboy."

Their most important next step tentatively agreed upon, they kissed. Tenderly at first, then with more and more passion. Until there was no longer any denying not just their physical need, but this life they were building together.

Blindly, they found their way inside the ranch house. Still kissing, traversed the stairs, and made love in the cozy comfort of his bed. Afterward, they clung together, savoring the closeness, yet knowing another very important decision had to be made.

"Cullen?" Bridgett prompted softly.

"Hmm?" Knowing he had never been happier, he buried his face in her hair, drinking in her unique fragrance.

"About Robby and Riot."

He drew back, heart pounding.

"I've changed my mind about that. I want us to foster-adopt them together so we can continue to be the real family we were meant to be, right from the start. With absolutely no interruption."

Another dream come true. Soberly he told her, "I want that, too."

She hugged him fiercely, the joy flowing between them, tangible. "Then it looks like we will be calling DCFS first thing tomorrow and amending that adoption petition, after all."

Epilogue

April 1, one year later

Cullen watched as Bridgett paused at the edge of the band-stand that had been set up on the Western Cross ranch lawn. Gorgeous as could be in a red party dress and heels, their baby on her hip, their dog at his side, she turned to Cullen and murmured, "Hard to imagine so much could have happened in so little time, isn't it?"

And yet it had.

Savoring the happiness infusing every corner of his life, he grinned back at her. Winked. "Well, hang on, dar-lin', because the best is yet to come."

Her eyes lit up in the way he loved. "Promise?"

He nodded solemnly. "I do."

They locked gazes as readily as they had already locked hearts. Knowing it was either proceed with the festivities or sweep her off to make love with her then and there, Cullen reined in his desire and caressed her cheek with the pad of his thumb. "So, what do you say, Mrs. McCabe? Ready to get this party started?"

She slipped her hand into his. "Let's do it, cowboy!" Together, they moved to the microphone at center stage and gazed at the circle of family and friends gathered in front of them.

As previously agreed, he talked first while caterers passed out glasses of champagne. "Bridgett and I want to thank you all for coming to help us celebrate the first anniversary of the miracle discovery that brought Bridgett and I and Robby and Riot all together." *And opened up our lives, and our hearts...*

Beside him, Bridgett wordlessly offered her support.

Ready to finally say all the things that needed to be said, he located the beaming matriarch and patriarch in this branch of the McCabe clan. "And first, in this very long list of people to whom we owe so much, I want to thank Mom and Dad. And, yes, I call Rachel and Frank that now, because they are both my parents and I love them both very much."

A ripple of appreciation went through the crowd. "To my brothers and sister, Dan, Jack, Matt, Lulu and Chase, for hanging in there and being my sibs even when I wasn't sure I needed any younger brothers, never mind a baby sister, in my life!"

Soft, knowing laughter followed.

When the hilarity died down, Cullen said, in all sincerity, "A special thanks to the entire Monroe clan, as well—" he paused to name them all in turn "—for welcoming me into their lives."

Emotional hoots followed.

Cullen looked over at the cowboys seated at the gingham-draped dinner tables. They were part of the Western Cross family, too. "I'd also like to thank everyone who helps me out on the ranch." He paused to list them.

"And Riot, the handsome mutt that accompanies me everywhere...and as all our wranglers can readily insist, has turned into one of the best darn cattle dogs who ever lived."

Hearing his name, Riot perked up and thumped his tail.

Cullen wrapped his free arm around Bridgett and brought her and their baby in close to his side. His voice turning as tender as his feelings, he continued his increasingly emotional toast. "I'd also like to thank Robby, who teaches me every day what it is to be a dad," he said, his voice cracking slightly. "And how spectacular it is to have a son."

He leaned over to buss the top of their little one's head. The one-year-old chortled happily and, a ham at heart, blew first Cullen and then his mommy affectionate, noisy kisses back, making everyone laugh.

Eyes misting, Cullen turned and looked deep into Bridgett's beautiful eyes. Knowing he could never say it often enough or well enough to convey all he felt, all he had discovered, he continued from the deepest recesses of his heart.

"And last, and most importantly of all, to my wife, Bridgett." He gazed lovingly down at her. "The woman who upended my life and stole my heart and showed me how to love with every fiber of my being," he managed, before his voice caught.

Taking a deep breath, he plunged on, reminiscing fondly, "All, mind you, while sharing with me the best three month courtship and nine months of marriage a couple could ever dream of having."

Tenderly, he lifted her face to his, and blotted the tears of happiness streaming down her face with the pad of his thumb.

Once again, they were completely in synch. "I adore you, sweetheart," he said gently.

Bridgett went up on tiptoe and kissed him. "Oh, Cullen, I adore you, too!"

Love flowed between them, fiercer than ever.

He bent his head and kissed her again while the baby

let out a whoop of delight and Riot gave a jubilant woof. The family and friends gathered round laughed, cheered and clapped. But all Cullen could focus on was how right everything finally felt. How...there was no other word for it...*destined*.

Eventually he drew back, knowing deep in his soul that their lives were now the way they were always meant to be. Bridgett felt it, too, he could see it in the way she looked at him every hour of every day.

"And now—as we all get ready to lift our glasses— Bridgett has a few words of her own to say."

Her cheeks taking on a rosy maternal glow, Bridgett handed off Robby to him and stepped up to the microphone. Looking more angelic than ever, she declared, "Multiple births don't just run in the McCabe clan. Twins run in the Monroe family, too. And now," she declared joyously, to one and all, "Cullen and I are going to have a pair of babies simultaneously, too!"

Elated, Frank stood. So did Rachel. The McCabes and Monroes and their spouses all followed. Soon everyone was on their feet, cheering wildly, raising their glasses.

"To our family, which is getting bigger and happier and more fulfilling every day," Bridgett toasted.

"Amen to that!" someone shouted. Glasses clinked. People sipped.

"You've made all my dreams come true," Cullen said, cuddling their son and drawing her close once again.

Bridgett looked up at him adoringly. And kissed him one more time. "Mine, too, cowboy," she whispered back, snuggling close. "Mine, too..."

* * * * *

MILLS & BOON

Coming next month

RESCUING THE ROYAL RUNAWAY BRIDE
Ally Blake

"Look," Will said, stopping to clear his throat. "I'm heading towards court so I can give you a lift if you're heading in that direction. Or drop you...wherever it is you are going." On foot. Through muddy countryside. In what had probably been some pretty fancy shoes, considering the party dress that went with them. From what he had seen there was nothing for miles bar the village behind him, and the palace some distance ahead. "Were you heading to the wedding, then?"

It was a simple enough question, but the girl looked as if she'd been slapped. Laughter gone, colour gone, dark tears suddenly wobbled precariously in the corners of her eyes.

She recovered quickly, dashing a finger under each eye, sniffing and taking a careful step back. "No. No, thanks. I'm... I'll be fine. You go ahead. Thank you, though."

With that she lifted her dress, turned her back on him and picked her way across the road, slipping a little, tripping on her skirt more.

If the woman wanted to make her own way, dressed and shod as she was, then who was he to argue? He almost convinced himself too. Then he caught the moment she glanced towards the palace, hidden somewhere on the other side of the trees, and decidedly changed tack so that she was heading in the absolute opposite direction.

And, like the snick of a well-oiled combination lock, everything suddenly clicked into place.

The dress with its layers of pink lace, voluminous skirt and hints of rose-gold thread throughout.

The pink train—was that what they called it?—was trailing in the mud behind her.

Will's gaze dropped to her left hand clenched around a handful of skirt. A humungous pink rock the size of a thumbnail in a thin rose-gold band glinted thereupon.

He'd ribbed Hugo enough through school when the guy had been forced to wear the sash of his country at formal events: pink and rose-gold—the colours of the Vallemontian banner.

Only one woman in the country would be wearing a gown in those colours today.

If Will wasn't mistaken, he'd nearly run down one Mercedes Gray Leonine.

Who—instead of spending her last moments as a single woman laughing with her bridesmaids and hugging her family before heading off to marry the estimable Prince Alessandro Hugo Giordano and become a princess of Vallemont—was making a desperate, muddy, shoeless run for the hills.

Perfect.

Continue reading
RESCUING THE ROYAL RUNAWAY BRIDE
Ally Blake

Available next month
www.millsandboon.co.uk

LET'S TALK
Romance

For exclusive extracts, competitions
and special offers, find us online:

f facebook.com/millsandboon

⊙ @millsandboonuk

𝕏 @millsandboon

Or get in touch on 0844 844 1351*

For all the latest titles coming soon, visit
millsandboon.co.uk/nextmonth